Pushing Back

Book One in the Boone Series

by Jim Hartsell

House Mountain Publishing

Copyright © 2016 by Jim Hartsell

Cover design by:
www.nickcastledesign.com

ISBN   978-1-7327549-0-4

Also by Jim Hartsell

The Boone Series:

Matching Scars (Book Two)
Keeping Secrets (Book Three)

Other Fiction:

Tango
Rock, Paper, Scissors
Journey

Children's Books:

The Box of Toys
Father and Sister Radish and the
        Rose-Colored Glasses
The Mountain Climber

Non-Fiction:

Glimpses
Sisyphus and the Itsy-Bitsy Spider

Chapter One

The air gets so thick here you can hardly draw breath sometimes. They tell me it's worse down in Memphis, but I don't hardly see how that could be. Going outside it just drags you down, and all you want to do is find a tree and a breeze. There's a creek up from the house, back in the woods, and in there's the coolest spot I've found. I go there whenever I can slip away, through the briars at the edge of the woods, stepping into the shade and heading for the one deep pool in the only part of the creek I know about. I want to go farther up and see what's on the Thompson's land, but Daddy says they don't like it when folks nose around. He says that they got their own business, just like we do, and I need to keep my ass off their land. Course that just makes me want to go that much more.

The path is one I made myself. I can see it, but that's because I know where to look for the signs. It's not a long walk from the back of the house up to the pool, but I'm pretty sure I'm the only one that knows about it. We don't like folks on our land either, and Daddy never comes up here. Hannah's only seven, and Momma, she don't go anywhere without Daddy saying it's all right. So I'm the only one that knows about it, at least as far as I know.

It gets cooler as soon as I get under the trees, and I can breathe a little better. Up ahead the light is soft and there's just enough space between the trees to slip through. I like it out here, a lot better than in the house or about anywhere else, I guess. When I hear a noise I don't recognize I stop quick, right next to a big tulip poplar, and wait. Might've been a bird, but I couldn't make it out, and now it's gone. I wait for another minute or so and then start moving again. It won't be long before Momma is looking for me to do some chore or other. She mostly does chores now or just sits and stares at nothing. She hasn't smiled in a long time, since two summers ago about this time, I think. That makes sense.

The pool is behind the next pile of rocks, big and mossy and slippery all the time, so I'm careful about getting down to the water. There's a rock I usually sit on, up at the head of the pool, where the water comes in from up on Thompson's land.

The pool's about six or eight feet across and a sloppy round shape; I don't like to get in it, doesn't seem right somehow, but I did once and it's about halfway up my thighs in the middle. Cold and clean. I stood there for a half a minute that day and felt like I was dirtying it somehow so I got back out and haven't been in since. I don't bring a pole, either, even though I've seen a couple of pretty big ones in that pool. They look like they've been around for a while, and unless we get hungry I'm leaving them alone.

We were close to hungry two years ago in the late fall; there wasn't any work for Daddy right then, and he and Momma never were all that good at saving money. That fall they used up what little bit they had saved. They're still paying, too. Hospitals and funerals cost, even if you don't want anything fancy. Daddy wanted to dig the grave in that little place off the back yard, really the only place on the farm that's close to being flat, but the law said he couldn't do that. Some kind of county thing or state thing, I never did know. Pissed him off something fierce; I've only seen him like that a few times. I mean, I see him mad plenty, almost every day it seems, but not like this. I thought we'd have bail and lawyer money on us too but Momma talked him down. I was surprised, cause usually when she tries to do that it just makes him madder, but I guess he was grieving in his own way and just didn't have the heart to fight. He's usually a hard fighter, better at that than anything else he does, that's for sure. This time he just kind of shrunk down and went on out of the courthouse and was waiting for us in the car when we, I mean

Momma, finished talking to the county people and we got ourselves out of there.

I don't like thinking about that. That was a really bad week, and I don't reckon any of us have gotten all the way over it. Maybe never will. I try to let it go for a minute and watch the gliders on the water. Fish must not be hungry right now; there's a dozen or more gliders, skittering over the top of the water, and nothing coming up from underneath to snap them up. Middle of the day never has been good fishing, though. Fish must nap until evening. I sure wish I could.

This is the best place I know. There's almost always a little breeze, and it's quiet here except for the birds and the squirrels and sometimes I'll see something else, maybe a bobcat, maybe a coyote. Hard to make them out in all the cover, but I guess they like it that way. I know I would. I lean forward with my elbows on my knees and my chin in my hands and just watch the water go by, going down to the French Broad and then the Tennessee and then the Mississippi and then the ocean. I've never seen the ocean except in school and on TV. One of these days I'd like to, but I hear there's no trees or hills close by and I don't know how I feel about that. Anyway, that's for later on.

There's that sound again, that I heard on the way up. I can't quite make it out, way off, clear like a bird call but only for a second. I sit real still and wait for it to come again but it never does, and all I can hear is the wind and the water. Judging by the sun on the rocks, it's time I should be going back. Give it another minute or two, I think. Can't hurt.

I must've gotten lost in my own thoughts; when I look again the square of sunlight is long and skinny and almost down to the water. I just about bust my ass getting off the rocks and over to the bank. If I'm not home before Daddy gets there there'll be hell to pay. I've still got a couple of bruises from the last time I wasn't where I was supposed to be when he thought to look.

Light is fading a little when I make it out of the woods, scratching my arm on the briars there at the edge. When I get to the yard and Daddy's truck isn't there, I realize I've been holding my breath. I let it out slow and loud and start across the yard to the house. My foot is on the steps when I hear the engine, way off down the valley, and I hope it's not Daddy, although it sounds like the truck. Whoever's driving that thing is royally pissed about something. Hurrying across the yard, I take the stairs two at a time and find Momma right where I left her an hour or two ago. It's Daddy all right. Damn, that was close. He pulls up into the front yard and jams on the brake, skidding up close to the house. He doesn't like it when he thinks we're spying on him, so I back off from the window and go back into the kitchen to wait with Momma.

I look over at Momma when I hear the truck door slam. She won't look at me, just stares off into space like she always does. I swear, she spends half of every day at that damned kitchen table, doing nothing. Looking around the kitchen, I see the stuff from breakfast still out on the counter. That milk's probably bad by now, but I grab it on the way across the floor and open the fridge and slide it inside. The dishes I leave alone; there's no time to do anything about that. I know from the sound of the truck door that somebody's going to catch hell tonight. Right now I'm about half scared for Momma and half really mad at her. Why hadn't she done anything about any of that? And I have to admit, I'm scared for me, too. No telling who's going to be on his bad side tonight. It won't be Hannah, I'm pretty sure about that. She's still little, and he lets her get away with all kinds of stuff. She's starting to take advantage of that, like kids do, and I've tried to tell her she'll pay for that sooner or later, whenever he figures it out. She just laughed when I told her that, but right now she's standing over there at the back door, and I can see the fear. We're all scared, all three of us, and what are we doing? Standing around like a bunch of damn cattle, waiting, waiting. I try to put myself back at the creek, sitting on that rock, looking down into the pool, and it works for a minute or so.

Then Daddy is in the house, and it's not working anymore. He comes in through the back door and Hannah barely gets out of his way, going flat against the wall like I used to when I was her age. He doesn't even see her, just moves past Momma and the table and doesn't even look at me when he goes by. He's down the hall and into the closet, and I see him grab the shotgun and the box of shells and he's back and out the back door and heading out to the truck. I don't even think about it; I head out after him, not knowing why or what I'm going to say or do.

Chapter Two

I stop at the corner of the house and try to stay quiet. After giving it a half a minute, I step out past the house so I can see the truck, still in the front yard. He's not behind the wheel.

So where did he go? I'm used to dealing with Daddy in his moods, had to get used to it, especially over the last year and a half or so, but not with a shotgun. This is different, in a really scary way. For a minute I think I'd be better off just going back inside and maybe hiding under my bed, but that doesn't last long. According to the law I'm not a man yet, but Daddy expects me to act like one, so I take another step out. Then another.

He's sitting on the tailgate, the shotgun across his lap, the box of shells right beside him. The sun is low now, right in his face when he looks down the road, and his eyes are almost shut against it. I can hear him talking to himself when I get to the front bumper.

"Bastards better not follow me up here. This is my home, goddammit. They better not come up here."

He keeps saying this over and over, his eyes never leaving the road.

It had been three or four hours since he had left the house. None of us knew where he had gone, but we never did, so that was nothing new. I think about asking, but as soon as I think it I know better. The mood he's in, I'm on thin ice just going out there. I hate this, I think. I take another step towards him.

He tenses and I think he's going to swing the shotgun around in my direction, but all he turns is his head. He turns far enough to see that it's me and then turns back.

"Come on out here, Boone. Sit down over on this side and watch the road up toward the Thompson's."

I asked Momma one time where I got that name; I was afraid it was after Daniel Boone and I thought that was really stupid. The truth was worse.

"Your daddy and me used to drink a lot of Boone's Farm wine. It was all we could afford, and your daddy hadn't learned how to make his own yet." She had kind of smiled to herself. "Well, anyway, you asked."

So I let all the other kids at school think that Daniel Boone was this big hero to my parents and they laughed and made fun but it could've been a lot worse.

I never told anybody the real story, and they didn't give me a middle name, so I couldn't go that way to get out of it. So I was Boone. I had already looked up about changing my name, I mean, who wants to be named after some kind of cheap wine? But I knew that wasn't going to happen until I hit eighteen and moved out on my own.

One time I made the mistake of telling Momma what a stupid name I thought it was and didn't know Daddy was just coming into the room. That wasn't the worst beating I ever got, but it was pretty bad.

None of us were safe from his black moods. Well, Hannah. Far as I know, he never laid a hand on her. Momma, me, Frankie, that was different. Sometimes it'd be a week or two between beatings, but, like I said, nobody got away clean. Part of it was liquor, I know that. Part of it was they treated him the same way they treated all of us. If you lived up where we did, in any of those counties just outside Knoxville, you were trash and people felt like it was all right to shit on you any time they wanted to. Daddy had one job after another, he'd take it as long as he could, and then some boss would say something that he just couldn't walk away from. He had pride, I'll give him that. Plus he'd stand up to anybody. It was that time leading up to his standing up for himself that was hell for us at home. He would bottle it up all day long at work, maybe stop for a few on the way home, and then one of us would say something or not say something or do something or not do it, and he'd blow. Sometimes we could tell by the way he took that last curve before he whipped into the driveway and up into the yard. Sometimes none of us saw it coming. A couple of times I saw Momma's hand tighten around the handle of the cast iron skillet she had on the stove, but she never swung it at him. I think if she had there'd be a grave for one of them out there behind the house, county or no county. I used to wonder sometimes which one of them would win if it really got down to it. She'd always back down, though. Always. Never pushed back.

And Frankie, well, I still can't talk about Frankie.

"What is it I'm watching for?" I break the silence. He's stopped that talking to himself he was doing when I came up. He doesn't turn, doesn't take his eyes off the road.

"Just tell me if you see anybody. Specially anybody you don't know."

"Even Ginny Thompson?"

The butt of the shotgun catches me in the stomach before I have a chance to tighten up. All the air whooshes out of me and I bend double, trying to keep from falling off the tailgate into the dust.

"Don't you understand English, boy?"

"Yes sir," I manage, but it comes out more of a croak than anything else.

He's already looking back down the road. "Get your head up, then. We'll be losing light soon."

I slowly get my wind back and we sit, not saying anything, until we can't see the mailbox down at the road and the first couple of stars are starting to show themselves in a sky that still has a little color.

"I'm hungry," he says to himself, like he doesn't remember I'm out there with him. "Reckon I'll go on inside."

I know better than to move just yet.

"You want me to stay out here and keep watch?"

I don't know whether that's the right thing to say or not. It's impossible to know one way or the other. I know that when I mentioned Ginny Thompson, the twelve year old that lives up the road, I got slammed in the gut. You never know with Daddy.

He looks over at me. "Nah, no need."

He doesn't seem quite as mad. Maybe the people he was looking for not showing up before sunset eased his mind some. Maybe if they, whoever they are, haven't come by now they're not coming. A part of me is dying to ask him who he's looking for and why they might be coming all the way up here, but a bigger part of me tells me to keep my damn mouth shut.

He hops down off the tailgate and I slide down, trying not to make any noise when I land, even if it hurts, which it does. He puts the tailgate up and heads off, shotgun in the crook of his arm, the box of shells in his crippled left hand. He has to hold the box against his stomach; he hasn't been able to close the fingers of that hand since the accident with the hay baler half a dozen years ago. The doctors had told him he was lucky to still have the hand. They couldn't give him back much control over the fingers, though, so it was more a claw than anything else. All this time gone by and he's still mad about that, still talks about the Trent family like they held him and shoved his hand in there on purpose. Everybody, including me, knew his sleeve got caught in the machinery and the oldest Trent boy had saved his whole arm, cutting that sleeve before it could pull him in up to the shoulder. Quick with a knife, that boy was, but Daddy, as far as I know, never thanked him for that. The Trents paid the hospital bills, too. I think he did mumble something to them about that, but it was hard for him.

And there's part of all that I understand, at least a little. Daddy never wanted to owe any man anything. They say pride is a sin, but I don't know. Daddy doesn't have much but pride, so I think I know why he hangs on to it so tight and gets so mad when he has to take a big swallow. I get that. I just wish us folks that have to live with him didn't have to suffer when he thinks he's lost face. I start to follow him toward the house.

He's limping again. I wonder if somebody on the job kicked his ass today and that's what this is about, but I know better than to bring it up. Ever since the baler thing he's had to take whatever job he can — I've seen him rig a piece of rope into a sling so he can carry heavier stuff — but I know there's a lot of young men out there that can work him into the ground, and they're the kind that would let him know it every day. Tomatoes are just coming in and just like every year he's mostly at the Wilcox place again, a big farm with greenhouses and fields full of plants. He's up against all those Mexicans that sneak across the border; he hates the sight of them. He told me once that those brown-skinned bastards never stopped for a break, just kept on, shaming all the good white folks around them. I wonder if that's who I was supposed to be watching for.

I give up thinking about it and start toward the house when, pretty far off, I see headlights.

Chapter Three

When I get inside Momma points to the hallway. Hannah is standing beside her, her face buried in Momma's shoulder, and I run past them down the hall.

I got a room to myself after Frankie and that's the door that's standing wide open; I remember it half closed, so I stop while I'm still in the hall and look inside.

Daddy's on his knees up on Frankie's bed, looking through the curtains. He must've seen the headlights too, or heard the engine noise. I stand there looking at him for a second, thinking of what Momma would do if she saw him on that bed. She hasn't let anybody touch it or any of his stuff.

It took a while, I remember, to get used to seeing all his stuff there every morning when I woke up. Lots of times I started to move it all down the hall to the closet, even got a box once, but I just couldn't do it. Momma was crazy with grief for the longest time;

we all used to think it wouldn't be that much of a surprise to find her hanging one day, but she never did that. She just died in pretty much every other way. It might have pushed her to it if I had packed away all Frankie's stuff, so I never followed through. I wanted to, though. She sure doesn't need to see Daddy like this, so I pull the door closed behind me. He turns at the noise.

"What the hell are you doing in here? I told you to wait outside."

I never know what to say when he does this, which is happening pretty often now. So I stay quiet.

"It's too late for you to go back out. Just stay there and be still."

I think, yeah, I can do that.

Daddy turns back to the window. The headlights are coming up the last hill before they're either going to the Thompson's or coming here. Well, there's old man Everett's house, but nobody goes there. Some people say the old man is sitting in there in his kitchen, face down in his last breakfast, but I know better. I've seen lights in that house, once just a couple of days ago. He's still in there. So this truck, I can tell from the lights it's a truck, might be going one of three places after it tops the hill.

The truck stops at the top of the hill.

It just sits there for what seems like forever, with Daddy getting more and more nervous and me getting more scared. Then it starts moving hard left and I remember the gate to the hayfield right next to ours. We can just see the taillights now and the headlights shining out over the grass that's close to ready for cutting. The taillights flare bright and then the backup lights come on.

The truck comes back out into the road and heads back the way it came, and I breathe out the breath I'd been holding. Daddy backs off the bed and just stands there in the middle of the room, like he doesn't know what to do next. Like he was all ready to defend his home and then the threat just went away all by itself.

I step aside when he whirls around and heads out of the room and then I go over and straighten the blanket on Frankie's bed and think about when Frankie would have done that himself. He was always the neat one.

Used to be you could draw a line right down the middle of the room and it would be like two different bedrooms, mine like the mountain wind just blew through and his like a magazine picture. He'd help Momma with the rest of the house, sometimes without her asking, but he was real particular about his half of the room. I try shaking my head to get back to right now. I don't like thinking about this stuff.

I can hear Daddy as soon as I step into the hallway.

"Dammit, Natalie, this kitchen is a godawful mess. What'd you do all day, just sit there? Where's supper? What the hell am I supposed to eat? Answer me, dammit!"

Hannah is out the kitchen door and into the hallway just ahead of the sound of breaking glass. She passes me, her eyes full of fear, and slams the door to her room. I think about joining her, but I know Momma needs all the help she can get. She may not even defend herself, and maybe Daddy won't hurt her if I'm in the room with them. I start down the hall.

The outside door slams and I speed up. When I get to the kitchen, there's a broken plate on the floor, the refrigerator door is standing open, and Momma is on her hands and knees in the corner of the room, blood running down her face from a cut across her forehead.

I stop and stare, try to take it all in. He's hit her before, I know that, she's even told me that, but it's always been bruises that she won't even show us and I only knew about when she forgot and rolled up her sleeves to do the dishes or bent down to pull a weed and I could tell by the way she grabbed at her right side that she had a bad bruise there on her ribs. He's never made her bleed before, at least not that I knew about, and I don't even go to check on her, I'm on my

way out the door. I can hear her saying, "Boone, don't
. . . ." and then I'm out in the yard.

I'm looking around for him and he's nowhere in
sight. Anger is building up in me and I can barely
keep from shaking and I look and there's nothing and
I turn full circle and still nothing and I can't do
anything if I can't find him. You've gone way too far
this time, I keep repeating, and the anger is still
growing and growing. Where is he?

There's a crash down at the barn, then another,
and I'm running that way not knowing what I'm
about to do but I know I have to do something. From
behind me I can hear Momma's voice, faint and torn
apart by the wind, and I hear my name but I don't
stop.

Then I'm at the big door on the side of the barn
and it's standing partway open. Inside it's dark, no
light at all, and I start to go in and I'm scared to go in
and I'm caught. I can't run away from this, not again,
and I can't make myself go in because of what he did
to Momma and he doesn't think much of me anyway,
he's told me so over and over, and will he hold back or
really lay into me?

He comes out of that open door at a dead run and
it looks like he's running right at me and then he's by
me and headed toward the truck. I freeze for a second
and then I'm right after him. And I wonder what the

hell am I doing? He's bigger than me, tough as a pine knot, and he's my Daddy.

Then I think about Momma on the kitchen floor and get white-hot mad all over again and I'm catching up to him because he's stopped. He's made it to the truck and he's got his hands on the hood of that old F-150 and he's just standing there, chest heaving. I stop when I'm about fifteen feet away from him and I shout, "Hey! What did you do to Momma?"

He doesn't answer me, just stands there, his breath coming more regular now. I take another step toward him, then another. Close now. One more step and I say, "Listen, you stupid old bastard, you can't —"

All I see is a blur when he swings around, his arm straight out, that claw of a left hand coming right at the side of my head, and then everything goes black.

I'm probably only out for about ten seconds. When I can focus again he's standing over me rubbing his left hand with his right. I start to get up and he puts his boot in the middle of my chest.

"Don't you move, boy."

When I start to squirm around he steps a little harder and I stop. I'm afraid he might break a rib or worse. He shakes his head and says, "You call a man a name like that and don't even think about what he might do to you? Next time it might not be your daddy, next time somebody might just crack that skull." He eases up some on my chest. "You understand, boy?"

I nod.

He takes his foot off me and motions me to get up. He doesn't offer to help, and I don't ask.

"You get on into the house and check on your Momma and sister. I plan to stay out here and keep watch for a while."

Not steady enough to stand just yet, I stay hunkered down for another half a minute and then try standing. I'm wobbly but I can stand and I think I can walk without stumbling. Turning toward the door, I take a few steps, then a few more, steadier ones. I'm almost to the step when I hear him, back behind me, still at the truck.

"Damn kid," he's talking more to himself than to me. "What the hell's the matter with him anyway? Frankie, now, Frankie wouldn't have turned tail like that after one good lick. He would've made a fight out of it. Reckon it's too late to try to teach this one anything. He'll just be a pussy all his life. Damn shame."

I start to turn around and go at him full speed, surprise him. I'm trembling, I'm so mad.

Then I jerk open the door and go inside to check on Momma and Hannah.

Next morning I've got a knot on the side of my head big as a hen's egg. Light was coming in the window, looks like it might be eight or so. I look toward the door and Hannah is standing there staring at me.

"Are you gonna get up?"

I nod and swing my legs over. My head hurts like hell and I'm afraid to look in the mirror and see what that knot looks like. I'm glad it's Saturday and I don't have to fight with Momma about going to school. No way I'm going around other people until this goes down some.

"Is Daddy gone?"

She looks at me like she's about to cry and then says, "He left just after, you know, just after — "

"I get it."

"Momma's gone too."

"What?" I get up quick and look for my jeans and then think the hell with that and head out into the hallway in my underwear. "What do you mean, Momma's gone too?"

Hannah is crying now, that kind of cry where the tears just run down your face one right after the other and you can barely talk. She just turns and heads for the kitchen.

I come into the kitchen and she's sitting at her place at the table. "I'm hungry."

I ignore her because of the note on the counter; the bowl I always use for my cereal is holding it down. For a second I'm afraid to look at it, but Hannah is watching me, so I pick up the paper and take it over to the window.

I read it to myself. It says:

Boone, I called my sister up in Bristol and
she came down this morning and took me back.
I'll send for Hannah soon as I can. Love you.
Momma

Then, way down at the bottom:

There's some money in the pantry behind the
tomatoes I canned last year.

That was it. Nothing about me, what am I supposed to do? I guess she's not going to send for me. I go to the door and look outside. The truck is gone. Both Daddy and Momma are gone. I turn to Hannah.

"I'm hungry," she says. "Where's Momma?"

"You want some of your cereal, or you want a piece of toast?" I need some time to think about her other question.

She says cereal and I take her into the living room and turn on the TV.

Then I go back into the kitchen and sit down. Then I go over to the shelves Momma always called the pantry and look behind the tomatoes. There's a plain white envelope there. I take it back to the kitchen table and take the money out and count it.

There's almost two hundred dollars here, and I wonder how long Momma's been doing this, one or two dollars at a time. So. I look around and think, I don't know what I'm supposed to do now. Already I can tell I'm kind of hoping that Daddy doesn't come back here. Then I think, he's your Daddy, Boone, what kind of talk is that? And he's Hannah's Daddy, and this is his home.

Then I think about Momma and how she just ran out on her own kids, and I'm white-hot mad at both of them now and then I think what the hell am I supposed to do now I'm only sixteen years old and that's old enough isn't it boy no it's not I'm just a kid well maybe it's time you stepped up and showed your Daddy you're not a worthless pussy like he says you are and how am I going to get Hannah to school on Monday 'cause there's no way I'm going back to school ever again and it's a long walk to the grocery and they just left me here and what the hell am I going to do now and the phone rings.

I walk over to it and look at the little screen. We got caller ID 'cause Daddy wanted to know who was on the other end before he decided if he wanted to be home or not. It's Curt, and I really don't want to talk to him right now. He's one of the only guys at school that doesn't treat me like trash, maybe because he's not much better off than I am, but right now I just can't. So I let it ring.

Hannah comes back into the room with her bowl and goes over to the sink.

"You want some more?" I ask. I have no appetite, but sometimes Hannah doesn't stop at one bowl.

She shakes her head. "Where's Momma?"

"She said in the note she was going to visit Aunt Claire up in Bristol. She might come and get you soon and let you visit too," I try to make my voice sound like nothing special is going on.

She looks me right in the eyes. "Is that what that note says?"

I nod. "Sure is."

She's looking at me like she knows something else is going on. Finally she says, "My cartoon's back on," and goes back into the living room.

After a piece of toast I go back into the bedroom and put my jeans and a tee shirt on. Then I sit down on the edge of the bed and think, what do I do now?

When I hear the truck pull in I remember the money and run as fast as I can to get it out of sight. I get it back in its hiding place and tear off the bottom of the note and throw it in the trash just before Daddy comes in. He's so drunk he can barely walk.

"Where's Natalie?" He holds onto the door with his good hand and looks around the room. If he notices my head he doesn't mention it.

"She's gone," I say.

"Like hell," he says, and looks like he's ready to hit me again.

I show him the note.

He looks at it hard, like he's having trouble reading it. Then he lets it drop on the floor.

"What sister?"

"I don't know, Daddy, I just found the note a few minutes ago. I don't know." I realize I'm shaking and sit down at the table. You stupid old man, I think. You're too drunk to remember Aunt Claire.

He looks at me suspiciously. "You telling me the truth, boy?"

I nod. Then, when I see him look toward the noise from the TV, I say real quick, "Hannah doesn't know anything either."

He looks in the living room. Hannah is still in her pajamas, eyes on the TV.

Then his eyes are back on me. "You better not be lying to me, you little shit." He wheels around and slams the door hard on the way out. I go to the door and see him get into the truck and make a big circle in the yard, almost hitting the dogwood tree, and then he's gone down the road.

I just want to go back to bed.

Hannah comes back in and says, "I'm going to stay in my pajamas all day today."

"That's fine," I say. "We're not going anywhere anyway."

"Was that Daddy?"

"Yeah."

"Was he mad?"

"Yeah."

"He's always mad, isn't he?"

"Yeah."

She shrugs and goes back into the living room.

"I'm going outside for a while," I say to her as she is leaving. She doesn't act like she hears me at all, doesn't say anything.

Chapter Four

The barn door is still standing partway open, like when I came out to look for Daddy. Seems like a long time ago, even though it was just last night. I go inside; it's easier to see now with the sunlight coming through the spaces between the wall boards. It's cooler in here than outside, where it's already starting to heat up for the day. August used to be my favorite month, til they started changing the start of the school year earlier and earlier. Now there's nothing in August but school. Not this year, I think. Maybe not ever again.

I breathe in deep; the smell of the place is so familiar to me. Curt and I used to come out here and play all those good guy bad guy games — army, cops and robbers, cowboys and Indians. Come to think of it, it's been a couple of years since he's been over here for anything. His daddy and mine never really got along, but we never let that bother us. Wonder what changed with him. Maybe it was high school; he got bigger and stronger and started that silly mustache and I'm still like a skinny kid, no hair except on top of my head. He started hanging out with the other jocks and, well, I guess that explains that.

It was fun out here when we were younger, though. Those two stalls over there were great hiding places for whichever one of us was the bad guy. I look up into the poles we used to hang tobacco on before Daddy hurt his hand and couldn't keep a patch going; Frankie and I would straddle the poles and Daddy would hand up the sticks, heavy and green, sticky with sap from the mature plants.

That pile of loose hay in the corner was a great place to rest when we were worn out from chasing each other all over the farm. We'd lay there and tell each other all kinds of lies and talk about how we couldn't wait til we were grown and could do whatever we wanted to whenever we wanted to. Boy were we wrong about that.

All of a sudden it's not such a great place to be and I can't wait to get out of the barn and away from all the memories. I know there's some really bad ones coming up and I need to find something else to think about.

I leave the barn and start walking back to the house and that's when I notice the old bicycle I used to ride everywhere. I haven't been on it in years, but I'm thinking now it'd be a lot better to ride to the store than walk. I go back into the house to get a rag and bucket to clean it up.

One tire still holds air, I don't know how, but the other one is flat and I don't have a pump. The rest of it looks okay, a little small for me, but I'm thinking just in case it ends up being me and Hannah or maybe just me I'll have to have something.

The closest house to ours is toward town, one of the Jenkins kids, I can't remember which one. I know they've got little ones and I think I saw one on a bicycle a couple of weeks ago. The Thompson's place, in the other direction, is half again as far and mostly uphill, so that's out.

There's old man Everett's place, between us and the Thompson's, but I can't see him having a pump. It's a lot closer than anywhere else, though, and I don't want to leave Hannah for too long. Don't want to leave her at all, as far as that goes.

Old man Everett. Nobody's seen him for years, except the kid from the IGA that takes a box of groceries up there every three or four weeks. Last time I talked to him, Stanley I think his name was, he said that he never saw the old guy either, just a quick look when he was back down off the porch of somebody picking up the box of food and carrying it inside. That's more than anybody else, though. His place is Halloween creepy, big trees with roots up on top of the yard and branches that hang real low and rub against each other when the wind comes off the mountain just right. It's a little place, kind of square, one of the ends has a window into what I guess is the attic. One time I was up in the middle of the night and saw a light through the trees that I could have sworn came from that high window. When I was a kid I was scared of that house, always rode faster when I had to pass it on the way up to the Thompson's. That's when some of the other guys started making fun of me, just 'cause I didn't want to hang around the Everett place.

Mr. Thompson had a bonfire for all the families that lived close by about four years ago. Daddy wouldn't go, so that meant Momma couldn't go, and Hannah was just about three, so me and Frankie went and it was pretty good. Mr. Thompson had bought a bunch of hot dogs and marshmallows and, even though I was too young, I knew that some of the older kids had some shine back in the woods and they kept sneaking away from the fire and coming back all smiles and barely walking. I thought then that I couldn't wait til I was older. That was before Daddy's accident and before what happened to Frankie. Things haven't been good like that for a long while now. I heard that they had another one of those bonfires last year but I knew better than to even ask Daddy about going.

Funny how this stuff works. Daddy got his hand all screwed up over on the Wilcox place, but they're related to the Thompsons, so in Daddy's mind it's all the same family and they're all to blame. It never has made any sense to me, but I know we used to be friends with the Thompsons and then we weren't anymore and I can't follow the creek up from the pool because it's on their land.

But old man Everett just has that little piece of land kind of between us and the Thompsons and there's the place I'm thinking about going. Chances are he won't have a pump and I'll end up going somewhere else, but I got nothing else to do right now.

I push the bike up the hill from our place and walk it back down the other side and start back up again. The Everett house is about halfway up this hill, there on the right. I can see the mailbox — G. Everett — and those trees in the front yard. I push into the driveway and lean the bike against the tree nearest the road and go up to the door.

The screen door isn't latched, so I open it and bang on the door.

"Mr. Everett? Mr. Everett? This is Boone, from down the road a ways. You might know my momma Natalie?"

No answer, no noise from inside.

"Mr. Everett? Hate to bother you, but I was wondering if you had an air pump, you know, like for a bicycle tire? Mr. Everett?"

Still nothing. I let the screen door go and it bangs against the wood. Oh well, I think, it was worth a try. I'm across the porch and on the first step when I hear the door open.

"In the shed out back."

The voice is thin and crackly, and when I turn around the door is closing.

The path around to the back of the house is barely there, choked with weeds and briars, but I push through without too much trouble and find the shed he's talking about.

It's covered in vines and the roof looks like it won't hold up for many more rains, but the door is clear and I pull it open. In the bit of light the open door lets in I see a chain hanging from the ceiling. I reach out and give it a pull.

When the lights come on I just stare for a minute. The place is dusty, and I can tell it doesn't get used much anymore, but there's a bench along one wall that must be six or seven feet long, with the shelf above it crammed full of tools — chisels and clamps and vise grips and screwdrivers and saws and squares and rulers and some stuff I don't recognize right off. I could spend some time in here, I think to myself. I could have some real fun in this place.

I eventually remember what I'm there for and start looking for the pump. The place isn't messy like a lot of tool sheds, where things are just thrown in any which way. The air pump is on the wall, hanging from a nail. I take it down and leave the light on when I go, figuring I'll just try the tire and bring it right back.

The tire holds air and I give the other one a few pumps just to firm it up, take the pump back, turn out the light, and close the door. I can feel him watching me from the house during this whole thing.

When I go back to the door to thank him, it's open just a crack and I can see him standing right behind it.

"I just wanted to say thanks for the pump, Mr. Everett."

"Welcome." His voice is thin and barely above a whisper, like he doesn't have much breath to spare on words. He closes the door and I take that as a sign I should leave.

Riding the bike home wasn't easy, since it had been so long, but definitely better than pushing. I made it back, no truck in the yard, Hannah still in the living room.

I start to go back outside.

"Momma called."

I stop and go back into the living room.

"When?"

"While you were gone." She hasn't taken her eyes off the TV.

"So what did she say? Is she okay?"

Hannah finally turns to me. "She said that Aunt Claire and Uncle Sammy were going to pick me up from school on Monday and I should pack my blue backpack like for a vacation." She turns back to the cartoon she is watching.

Well, there you go, I think. You're on your own with him now, Boone. Thanks, Momma.

I'm halfway across the kitchen when Hannah says, "She said to tell you she'll call you."

"Okay."

I can't think of anything else to say. So she's getting Hannah out of here, that's a good thing. What's she going to say when she calls, if she calls? Hang in there, Boone?

Hannah is standing in the kitchen doorway.

"And she said for me to bring Frankie's picture and his drawings." She goes back into the living room and sits down.

She's not coming back, I think. She's really going to do it this time.

Last year, when we were all still trying to get our feet back under us after what happened to Frankie, she and Daddy really got into it. She was giving as good as she got with him that day, which hasn't happened since, and she finally ran into their room, slamming the door behind her, and came out a few minutes later with a suitcase in her hand. I'd never seen Daddy like he was when he saw that suitcase, and I've sure never seen him that way since that afternoon. He was begging her to stay, saying, "I'm sorry, sorry," over and over, promising it would never happen again, that he would never say the kind of things he had said to her, that he would never blame her again. She made him beg for a good hour or two before she finally gave in.

That night she made the best fried chicken I can remember eating and a banana pudding with meringue about an inch thick on top. I reckon she told Daddy what to get and he was off to the store like it was some kind of race and he had to be sure he won it. They laughed and whispered to each other like a couple of teenagers and went for a walk after supper when it was just darkening outside and didn't come back til it was full night. I remember them walking across the field in the moonlight, bumping into each other, still laughing and talking low.

That lasted about three days, and pretty soon it was back to normal.

Chapter Five

On Monday I make sure Hannah has everything she needs in her backpack and walk her down to where the bus turnaround is. "Bye," she says and gets on the bus.

"Bye," I say.

When I start back to the house, I only get about halfway there when I see the truck. I'm sure it's Daddy's, but I don't want it to be. I start running up the last hill before our property so I can get a look. There is a grove of cedars on the same side of the road as our place, and I duck into them and work my way up to a spot where I could see.

It's him, all right. I get there just as he is getting out of the truck. I know he would expect me and Hannah to be in school and Momma to be at home. He gets out of the truck and heads straight for the back door. He isn't gone more than two minutes.

He comes out carrying the shotgun in the crook of his arm and I panic, thinking about the note she left.

41

Had it said where she was? Is he going after her? He doesn't turn toward the truck, though. He goes the opposite way, toward the barn. I see him go in, weaving a little, and then I hear a noise that sounds a lot like a shotgun.

For a long minute I just stand there, staring at the house and the truck and the barn. Then I start back to the road and down to the house, taking my time. I am really afraid of what I am pretty sure I'm going to find. I go into the house first.

The place is a wreck. How could he have done so much damage in just a couple of minutes? Kitchen drawers are yanked out and their contents slung across the counter and the kitchen floor, the couch in the living room is shoved sideways, a picture of Momma and Daddy is on the hall floor, glass shattered. The door to their bedroom is wide open. It's been a long time since I have been in that room. I don't go in; I just look inside. The mattress is crooked, clothes are everywhere, and, over on the far wall, a mirror that somebody had put a fist into. Written on the glass in lipstick, still legible across the cracks, are two words: No More.

I didn't even know Momma owned lipstick.

If the house was a mess, the barn is much, much worse. I know it is Daddy only because I had seen him go in, because his face and a lot of his head is gone, thrown all over the barn. He must've used a slug instead of shot.

I go back into the house and push the couch back into place. Then I sit down on it and started trying to figure out what the hell to do next.

Sorrow was what I am supposed to be feeling, I know that, but there are no feelings at all. I look around the living room; I could see the mess in the kitchen from where I was sitting. All this will have to be cleaned up. Or will it? What would be the point? I don't know.

Eventually I get up and go back outside, leaving the house for another time. There are no cars or pickups in the yard, no police cars, no sign that anybody heard it or if they did, thought it was anything other than a normal sound. It was a normal sound, I think to myself. I don't think about what I'm getting ready to do.

I clear out enough space at the front of the barn to make room; there was enough hay on the floor to catch the blood and pieces of Daddy, so the floor cleans up easy. The keys are in his pocket, and I get a little blood on my hand getting them out, but not as much as I'm going to. I wipe my hand on my jeans and hope the blood will come out. I like these jeans.

The truck is already pointing toward the barn, more or less, so it'll be easy to get it out of sight. I'll worry about what to do with it later. I don't think

Daddy owes anything on it, so the bank won't be sending anybody around.

The piece of land where Daddy wanted to bury Frankie is behind and east of the barn, up toward the Thompson place, and circled in trees, redbuds mostly. Pretty in the spring, that's why Daddy wanted the grave there. Guess he's going to get his wish about that, county be damned.

The ground is not too hard; the rain two weeks ago was a real soaker, and even though the yard has dried out enough to drive on the digging is easy. It's not a fancy grave I'm digging, and there won't be a headstone, but nobody's going to be visiting except maybe me and Momma and Hannah, and maybe not anybody at all. Daddy's people are from over in North Carolina, and he hasn't seen or talked about them in years. Where he was working, people come and go all the time, and nobody in town really cared for him; he was alway on a hair trigger, and folks don't like that much.

I don't know exactly how deep to make it, but I go down about three feet. The clay gets hard to deal with about halfway down, and I have to switch to the pickax. When I finish, there's enough rocks in the pile to cover the body if I carry a few, and this piece of land has always had plenty of rocks.

I go back into the barn; it's mid-afternoon by now, still plenty of light, but I need this to be done,

44

finished. I look down at what used to be Daddy and say, "You son of a bitch. You coward. What if Momma had been the one to find this?" Suddenly I'm exhausted, but I know I can't stop in the middle of this.

There is an old tarp draped over the side of one of the stalls. I spread it out and drag the body and the bloody straw onto it and get it to the gravesite and roll it in. Daddy tumbles into the grave and ends up face down. I fight the almost uncontrollable urge to laugh; he doesn't have a face, not anymore. That's when I notice the outline of his wallet. I had forgotten to go through his pockets. Feeling like a grave robber, I jump down into the hole and toss the wallet up onto the ground. There's nothing in any of his other pockets, and I scramble out, glad to be done with that part. The tarp is useful for hauling hay and other signs of what happened from the barn to the hole, but I don't want it around anymore. When I have everything I can see, I drag everything out, dump it in the hole, and toss the tarp in on top of it all and weight it down with rocks.

Filling in the hole completely wears me out. There's too much dirt, so I mound it up and try to even it as much as possible. When I finish, I take a step back and think that it needs something to camouflage it. Hay is all I have, so I get some more from the barn and scatter it over the dirt and toss a few rocks on top for good measure. To me it stands out like a neon sign at night, but I know that nobody comes through here. Daddy made it clear when we moved onto the place how he felt about trespassers, and most people here just want to mind their own business anyway.

I go back to the barn and pull the big door shut. I carry the shotgun back to the house and remember as I'm climbing the steps that I forgot to eject the shell. I had meant to toss it in the hole too. I'll toss it out into the woods later, I decide, and take the shotgun back to the closet.

The house takes a while, mainly because I'm in no hurry anymore. While I'm cleaning, I think about what I just did. No second thoughts, no remorse, just going over the details to make sure I didn't leave anything out. If anybody does come asking for Daddy, which I don't see happening, I can say that when I got back from taking Hannah to the bus the truck was here but Daddy was gone.

And that won't be a lie.

The one place I don't go is their bedroom. I can't see going in there, not yet. Momma hasn't been gone all that long, and she might come back anytime and she would wonder if things were different. So I concentrate on the rest of the house, and get everything more or less back to the way it was before Hannah and I left for the school bus.

There isn't much in the refrigerator, but on one of the cabinet shelves I find a can of black beans and some salsa that Hannah had talked Momma into buying the last trip, even though she almost never bought things like that, said we couldn't afford them. So supper is black beans and salsa with some onions on top. I love onions, and there was a big Vidalia that hadn't been cut yet. Monday night there isn't much on TV, but I spend the whole evening watching one show after another. Before I realize it it's midnight and I haven't moved off the couch. I stretch out on the couch, change channels one more time, and I'm asleep before the first commercial.

That lasts about an hour before the dreams start. I keep waking up over and over, because I'm seeing Daddy lying there with half his head gone and blood everywhere, and then I'm out digging that grave, over and over, and then it starts all over again. So my first night alone in the house doesn't go so well.

The next morning I wake up and it's almost ten o'clock. I had been awake so many times during the night that when I finally wake up for good it takes me a minute to get my bearings. When I remember yesterday, I get so queasy I'm afraid I'm going to throw up and there's nothing on my stomach. I sit up and try to settle down and succeed, mostly. There's cold cereal in the pantry and I have three or four handfuls of that and make some instant coffee.

Carrying the second cup into the living room, I sit down on the couch to try to figure out what to do next.

I hate the thought of going through Momma's stuff, but I feel like I need to. I want to just keep going the way I was last week, staying out of Daddy's way and going to school. The fact is I know I can't do that, Daddy's not coming back ever and Momma's never gone this far before, taking Hannah a hundred miles away, so she may be gone for a while too. Nobody but me to take care of me.

Funny how I know I'm supposed to feel bad about Daddy and don't. Momma I miss a little, but who I really miss is Hannah. I think about not seeing her again and all of a sudden I'm crying, crying hard, rocking back and forth and wailing like an old woman at a funeral.

This goes on for a while, longer than I want it to, but I can't seem to stop. Finally it sort of wears itself out and I go into the kitchen and splash water on my face. Then I start trying to clean things up in the house, better than I did yesterday. The living room is easy, just a few things thrown around, and there's not much in there anyway. Kitchen's a little harder, even after what I did yesterday. It takes me the rest of the morning and on into the afternoon to get all the rooms except Momma and Daddy's bedroom fixed up. Hannah's is easy; guess he didn't go in there.

Same with my room; I didn't sleep there last night, so it's pretty much like it was before all this started. I decide to give Momma and Daddy's room one more day. Can't make myself go in there yet.

I go back out into the barn to have another look around; it looks like I got everything, which surprises me. I wasn't really thinking yesterday, just doing. The blood spatters on the walls are dry and kind of the same color as the old dirty wood. I think if I tried to clean all that up it would sort of stand out. So I leave it alone and look around one more time, kick the dirt and hay around so it doesn't look like I cleaned anything up. It's been a few years since anybody's had any cattle or pigs in here and everything is dusty and old and has that musty smell. I try to look at it like I've never seen it before and it doesn't look like anybody blew their brains out in here. The thought makes me want to throw up and I get out of there quick.

I think about school for a minute and wonder if I can get away with just not going back. I know a couple of guys who did but they were one year ahead of me. I'll figure out that later. Not going today, that's for sure. I walk around the barn and head over to where I dug Daddy's grave yesterday. It jumps out at me as soon as I get past the trees, like a big scar in the earth. I turn around quick and go back the way I came. There's still enough time left this season for

49

some grass to grow there, I say to myself. Maybe I should plant a tree or a bush or something. Kudzu, I think, and that makes me smile a little. Kudzu would cover that up in a heartbeat. Heading for the barn, I get the shovel and go across the road to the fencerow; it's always covered this time of year. I follow it along til I get to a natural break in the mass of leaves and vines and dig out a section of roots, trying to keep enough dirt around them. My knife is almost too small to do much good on the vines tangling in the woven wire fence, but I finally get a clump loose and start back to the house.

Mr. Thompson goes by in his new Chevy pickup and gives me a look; he doesn't stop and I don't have to explain why I'm transplanting something most everybody would like to see die all the way back to the roots and stay that way. Shit, I think, I need to be more careful about this kind of stuff.

I make it back to the house without anybody else seeing me and take the kudzu out to the burial mound and plant it right in the middle. Putting the shovel back in the barn, I get a bucket and give it a drink of water. I need this stuff to grow and grow quick.

It's getting close to sundown now, and I head back to the house for my second night alone. Actually feels kind of good, not having anybody to answer to about anything. Wonder how long this will last? As soon as

I think that, I know how to get an idea. Part of me still doesn't like the notion of snooping around in Momma's room, but if I knew how much stuff she took with her it might give me an idea.

I almost quit before I even get through the door, but I force myself across the threshold into the room and start looking around. After only a couple of minutes I switch on the light. The place is an absolute wreck. At first I think it's going to be hard for me to find out anything, and then I remember that Momma and Daddy each have a suitcase. So did Momma take one suitcase or both of them? If she packed both of them that might be just about everything she has, and that might mean she's not coming back.

The only place in the bedroom to store those suitcases is under the bed, so I get down on my hands and knees and hold up the quilt that blocks my view.

Nothing. Just two rectangles where there is no dust or loose socks or anything. They're both gone, and I think that means so is Momma.

The phone rings and I try to get to it but I can't get up and get there in time, so I have no idea who was trying to call. Curt? Momma? Somebody for Daddy? I stand there in the kitchen looking at the phone like it's going to tell me something. This thing used to give me a list of who had called, back about twenty-five numbers, but that button hasn't worked

51

in a while. I think about replacing it and then remember that I don't have any money besides what Momma left me.

And that gets me thinking. What the hell am I going to do about food and electricity? We're on a well and septic tank, so I don't have to worry about water unless they shut off the power. I realize I don't have any idea how much that kind of thing costs. What is our electric bill? Is it due? Past due? I don't even know where to look for that.

I don't think I like this part of being on my own much.

Chapter Six

Not really hungry, I go into the kitchen anyway because it's that time of day. The refrigerator is close to empty but there is some stuff and I guess most of it is still good. Maybe I should eat the old stuff first, I think, but I really don't have an appetite right now. So I close the refrigerator and go into the living room. There's nothing on TV but I sit down in front of it anyway and click through the channels. After while I settle on a movie I've only seen three or four times so it doesn't matter that it's already a half hour into it.

When the movie's over I'm not tired, but I know I should get some sleep. Then I think, why is that? Nobody here to tell me when to eat or drink or go to bed or get up, so why am I worried about that?

The notion that there's nobody here to tell me when to eat or drink reminds me that there's nobody here to tell me what not to drink either. Daddy always kept some shine out in the barn and thought none of us knew where it was, but I knew. Wonder how much is there?

The flashlight throws a dim beam out across the yard. Batteries must be getting low. One more thing to have to think about buying, but I don't worry about that right now. It's enough to get me out to the barn and into the second stall. Toward the back is a pile of hay that is a little taller than the rest of the bedding. I brush it aside and uncover the wooden box, pick it up, and carry it back to the house. No reason to leave it out there anymore.

The box is heavy and makes clinking noises when it bangs against my thighs. It's hard to carry and hold the flashlight, but I manage to get to the house without dropping either one. I set the box down, open the kitchen door, pick up the box, and carry it inside. The screen door bangs shut behind me and I kick the wooden door closed with my heel. When I set the box on the kitchen table, I realize I'm breathing hard, and I also realize I'm kind of excited. Never tasted shine before although, like the other guys at school, I always told everybody that I had. Well, Boone, I say to myself, that's about to change.

There are four jars in the box, three of them full, the other one about two-thirds full. I take a glass from the cabinet to the right of the sink over to the table and unscrew the jar lid, pour the glass about half full, and look at the jar. Still about half full, maybe a little more than half. I put the jar back in the box and close it. Then I pick up the glass and raise it to my nose.

Doesn't smell bad at all. Daddy used to say he only bought the good stuff, and once he mentioned a guy's name — Taggart, Talbot, something like that — from over across the ridge. I have no idea of how to go about buying shine or how much it cost, and decide to worry about that later. Carrying the glass with me, I go into the living room and sit on the couch. Settling back, I take my first real drink of shine.

I manage to set the glass down on the floor before the coughing gets completely out of control. My eyes are watering, everything is burning from my lips back, and I'm fighting like hell to keep from throwing up all over the floor. It takes forever to get everything back under control, and I sit there for a minute, wiping my eyes and thinking, what the hell was that I just drank? Maybe that wasn't shine after all; maybe it was something that was killing me from the inside out right now. Nobody would find my body for days, weeks maybe. I stand up to go to the phone and immediately sit back down. The room is moving, tilting, and I'm trying to make it stop,

Eventually everything settles down and I pick up the glass and look at it. Damn, that's strong stuff. I raise the glass to my lips, thinking what are you doing you fool, and take a very small sip.

This works much better, and the room doesn't go directions it shouldn't go. I set the glass back on the floor and lean back. Okay, I think, okay. This is for sipping.

By the time the glass is almost empty I'm enjoying the late night infomercials and wishing I had a credit card so I could buy one of everything. Guess maybe it's a good thing I don't have one. I'm still not hungry but one of my buddies at school told me that you should always eat something when you're drinking. I don't know what goes with shine so I go into the kitchen and look around. After staring at the refrigerator for a while I decide on a hunk of cheese and some sliced tomatoes. The knife almost gets away from me a couple of times but I get a plateful and go back into the living room.

I understand how Daddy can get so, well, out of control on this stuff, but I don't get why he's so mad when he's loaded. Maybe there's, or was, something besides the shine going on. I try to think about it but pretty soon I forget what it was I was thinking about and I'm looking for something else on TV. I don't remember what was on when I fell asleep.

Six hours later I'm awake and hurting. I've never done anything like that before, plus I slept sort of halfway sitting up on the couch, plus I buried my Daddy after he blew his head off, plus Momma and

Hannah are gone, probably for good. I lie there for an hour or so just trying to figure out what to do first.

What I decide on is breakfast. Or lunch, or whatever meal this is. The rest of the dry cereal later, I'm feeling a little more like normal and feeling like I need to go to the store. There's not much in the kitchen and I need to at least do something. I get Daddy's wallet out of the pile of stuff on the kitchen counter and take everything out.

He's got a driver's license and $24.00 and a couple of slips of paper with names and numbers on them; I set those aside to look at later. The only other thing is a lottery ticket. I look at it and see that it's for this week's game. I have no idea how the lottery is played or what the numbers mean or anything about it, but I put it aside too. I'll have to decide who to ask about this stuff.

And that's about it. Not much useful here except for the money. And maybe the lottery ticket. I decide to ride the bike down to the store and pick up a few things with Daddy's last bit of money.

The store is a mile and a half away, an easy ride for somebody who is used to riding and is not hung over. So I have a little trouble getting there. I push a cart through the aisles and get cereal and bread and baloney and cheese and a couple of two liter size Thunderstorm Sodas. Soda with a Kick. Momma never let us buy that, too much caffeine, she'd always say. It comes to a little less than $14.00, so I have some left before I have to get into Momma's money.

The poster in the window says that the lottery drawing is Friday and the top prize is 48 million dollars. I don't even let myself think about that, just get on the bike and pedal back to the house, the bag hanging off the handlebars.

With food in the house, I move to the next thing I need to deal with. The electric bill is somewhere in this house, I just don't know where, and I need to find out whether or not it's been paid or not and how much it is. Momma never had a checking account and Daddy never had any money, so the two hundred dollars I have is it until I can come up with something else.

When I finally find where Momma kept all the money stuff, in a drawer in the kitchen with recipes and stuff like that, I breathe a little easier. The next bill isn't due for another three weeks; must've not come in yet.

Over the next two days I change my mind about a dozen times about Daddy's grave. I decide to leave it the way it is and let the kudzu take that whole little field, and then I think I should plant a tree or something, and then I think why should I do anything for that nasty old drunk and then I'm all weepy 'cause I'm all alone and then I'm back to leaving it the way it is. I don't know what I'll end up doing, but it nags at me something fierce. Nothing from Momma or Hannah or Aunt Claire, and pretty soon it'll be a week.

Friday comes and I turn on the TV to the channel that has the lottery results. I do not win the 48 million dollars.

What I think I win is $400.00. I don't know how to play or how to read this but four of the numbers match and I think that's what the chart they show says gets $400.00. It goes by too fast for me to be sure, but if that's true then I'm in a lot better shape than I thought I was. I need to ask somebody to check this out for me.

I can't ask Curt; he'd make me give him half just for answering the question and he probably wouldn't know what he was talking about. Nobody around here would just tell me; they would want to know how I got the ticket, and if I took it to the store they might think I stole it from somebody. So I think I've got all this money and I don't know how to get it.

Then I think of Mr. Everett.

Would he help me with this? I don't know. I've always been a little scared of that house, even before the other kids warned me about it. And when I went up there to use the air pump I felt like he was watching me out the window the whole time I was in the shed out back. He still scares me a little but he's the only person I can think of to help with this.

Saturday morning I ride up to the Everett place and lean my bike against one of those monster trees and go up on the porch. The screen door is unlocked, like before, and I pull it open and knock on the glass pane in the wooden front door.

"Mr. Everett?"

No answer, just like before.

"Mr. Everett? It's Boone again, from down the hill."

The door opens a crack.

"Pump's right where you left it. Get your bike off my trees."

The door closes.

I knock again.

"Mr. Everett? It's not about the pump."

The door opens again.

"I said get your bike off my trees."

I turn and look at the bike, then turn back.

"Yessir, I'll do that right now."

I go down and take the bike over to the tire tracks heading back alongside his house and lay the bike down. The kickstand never did work on that bike, broken spring or something, so I don't bother with it.

I return to the front door.

"Is that okay?"

"What do you want?"

I tell him about the lottery ticket and how I think I may have won some money.

"Get your daddy to take care of it."

He starts to close the door.

"He's gone. Momma too. They run off after a big fight."

That was sort of true.

"You by yourself down there?"

"Yessir."

"How long?"

"Just a week."

He opens the door a little more.

"You got the ticket?"

"Yessir."

"Give it to me."

Now I don't know what to do. If I hand him the ticket I may never see it again and there goes that money. He clears his throat. It sounds like gravel in an old tin can.

"What's the matter? Don't trust me? Then what'd you come up here asking questions for?"

The door closes again, hard this time.

I knock on the door again. It opens just a crack, like before.

"What?"

"Listen, Mr. Everett, I'm sorry. I don't know what to do with this thing. Here," and I push the ticket through the crack in the door. He jerks it out of my hand and slams the door.

Well, that's that, I think. Four hundred bucks gone. I turn to go and the door opens again.

"Come back tomorrow."

I shrug and head on down to my bike and ride home slow. The phone is ringing.

"Hi."

"Hey, man, it's Curt. You sound like shit. Are you sick?"

Hell, yes, I'm sick, I think to myself. Might as well have set fire to that damn ticket. "Yeah, feel like shit. What do you want?"

"Don't be an asshole, man, I just wanted to tell you about a test coming up day after tomorrow. It's math, you might actually be passing math. Thought you might want to . . . Never mind, see you sometime."

"No, man, listen, sorry, I feel like I'm about to throw up all the time, thanks for the heads up, if anybody asks tell them I'll be back when this is over."

"Sure, no problem." He sounds pissed and hangs up. I don't blame him. Probably the only guy in school that doesn't treat me like trash and I'm blowing him off. I start to call him back and think why bother? I pour another shine, not too much this time, and stretch out on the couch.

The next day I go back to Mr. Everett's place, I don't know why. It's about one in the afternoon when I knock on his door.

It opens right away, just a crack, and an envelope comes through. I grab it; it feels heavy, and when I look inside, it's full of twenties.

"Had to give the kid twenty dollars to cash it in for me," the thin voice says from behind the door. "The rest of it is in there." He starts to close the door.

"Wait," I say. I can't believe that I've got almost four hundred bucks in my hand. "Don't you want some for, you know, your trouble? Just let me give you a— "

"Don't insult me, kid," his voice is a little angry. "Just say thank you and get out of here."

"Yeah, I mean, thank you, Mr. Everett, thank you."

The door is already closed.

I go back home and add the money to what Momma had in her envelope, then take it out and spread it out over the kitchen table and look at it. Then I stack it up and count it, and then count it again.

Five hundred and ninety-one dollars.

I put two hundred of it in my pocket and look around for a place to hide the rest. Two hundred back in the envelope in case Momma shows back up and needs it, I decide, and put the rest of the money in my top drawer with my socks and underwear.

I need to get back to my place up by the pool. I haven't been there since, well, in a week now. It's calling me, cool and quiet, just what I need right now and maybe forever, but right now for sure. I start to look for Momma to tell her where I'm going and then remember. No one to tell.

The little field where Daddy is buried is on the way, and I decide I can't stay away from that part of the farm forever. When I round the trees it still rattles me to see it, but it looks like the ground has settled some. If it'll go down a little more it'll be the same as the rest of the field and maybe I won't need the kudzu. For now I leave it alone, walk wide around it, but close enough to see that the kudzu is growing. Like there was any doubt. That stuff'll grow anywhere.

Stepping into the woods is like leaving the world behind. I think briefly that I should have brought some shine with me, but that doesn't last long. This place doesn't need anything. The path to the creek and my pool is clear to me and I follow it, hurrying a little as I get closer.

The noise comes to me faint on the wind, but clear, like a bell that doesn't fade out but keeps sounding. Then the wind shifts and I lose it, and it stays quiet the rest of the way to my spot. Nothing else disturbs me, nothing intrudes, the sound of the water and the cool of the stones draw the tension and worry right out of me, and I have time to think of nothing in particular. I stay until the light starts to fade and I remember I didn't bring a flashlight, and, even though I'm familiar with the trail, I'd rather travel it with some kind of light.

There are no lights on in the house; I had not left any on because I didn't know how long I would stay out there. The day is fading fast, just enough light for me to get into the house and turn on some lights. A fried baloney and cheese sandwich and a glass of Thunderstorm Soda, and I realize I didn't buy anything that could pass as dessert. I make a mental note to get some ice cream, now that I've got some extra cash.

The weekend passes, and the next week also. I decide to go to school a couple of days to keep my name off the shit list with the truant officer; next year he won't even bother, but this year he might, and I don't want any visitors. Curt must still be pissed at me; he gives me half a wave when he sees me on Tuesday and sits with some other guys at lunch, leaving me at a table by myself. Fine by me, I say to myself, and then I hear, "Mind if I sit down?"

When I look up it takes me a minute. We used to call Nancy "ironing board", as in flat as an ironing board, so it's really not surprising that I don't recognize her right off. She is definitely not flat anymore, but she still has those glasses that keep slipping down her nose and when she smiles it's easy to recognize her. She had braces put on toward the end of last year, and they are still there, you can barely see her teeth. Not somebody the guys have ever been interested in, which I guess makes her my equal; girls never have been all that interested in me. Too short, too skinny, funny shaped head, I know I'm the least good-looking guy around.

"Nah, I don't mind," I say, and she sits down opposite me.

There's a long silence, both of us looking at our school lunches, and I finally say, "Want to guess what that shit is on your tray?"

She smiles a little, not enough to open her mouth, which I understand with the braces and all. "I don't think it's actual shit," she says, and I grin in spite of myself.

"Guess you're right," I say.

Then there's another long silence, and finally she says, "I'm going to take a chance here and see what it tastes like."

"You first," I say, and she picks up a fork.

"Together," she says.

So I pick up my fork and she says, "On three."

When she gets to three we both get a forkful; it's pretty tasteless and I say so.

She nods. Another silence, for some reason they're getting less awkward. I take a few more bites and push the rest of the food around on the plate, then drop my fork in the middle of the glop and stand up.

66

"Had all I can stand, Nancy. See you later."

She looks up at me. "You've been out a few days. Feeling better?"

"Yeah, some kind of stomach thing." Shine'll do that to you, I think but don't say out loud.

"Okay, feel better," she says and looks back down at her food, still in separate piles on her tray.

"Thanks," I say and head off to dump the tray.

As I'm leaving the cafeteria, I take one look around the room. Nancy is watching me, staring really, and Curt is still with his group. He catches my eye and points to Nancy and then makes a loose fist with his left hand and pushes his right middle finger in and out, in and out. He and his buddies laugh, and one of them makes humping motions against the table.

Nancy follows my look over and sees the show. She goes beet red and gets up, leaving her tray, and runs out of the cafeteria. Curt and his crew are falling all over themselves laughing, the rest of the students are looking at them, and the cafeteria monitor is on his way over. The look on his face tells me this is not the first time he's had to deal with this group of assholes.

Last year I would have been right in there with them, but with everything that's happened to me lately, I just feel like I can't be bothered with that stuff right now. I feel a twinge of sympathy for

67

Nancy; all she did was sit down with me at the lunch table. I can imagine the hell she'll be going through for the next week or so. I make up my mind right then to stay the hell away from her. I don't want to defend her and I sure don't want to go up against those guys, but I know I don't want to draw any attention to myself. I just want to show up often enough to keep everybody off my back; I've got enough stuff to worry about without the school trying to get in touch with Momma or Daddy for a conference.

Chapter Seven

Nothing happens the rest of the day and I head home. On the way back to the house I decide to try to make it to school two or three days a week. That should make everybody but me happy. I'll just need to stay away from Curt and his gang and Nancy, well, I don't know what I'm going to do about that.

The next morning I don't wake up until school has started, so I decide to skip, and it feels great to just make up my mind on the spur of the moment like that. The downside is I'm finding out just how lousy pretty much everything on TV is. If we, I mean I, had some of those premium channels, things would be different, but I don't know how much more they would cost and I haven't called yet to find out.

The truck catches my eye one morning when I'm out in the barn checking to see if Daddy had any other hiding places for liquor. That part is a total bust, nothing in there that I can find, but looking at the truck starts me thinking. Why should I wear myself out on that bike when I can drive?

The keys are still in the ignition from the night I pulled it into the barn, so I slide behind the steering wheel and turn the switch. Nothing. I try again, and again nothing. I take the key out and put it back in and turn it again, and this time it comes to life for a second, dies, and then the engine turns over very slowly, slower every time it turns, and then there's a cough and another and the motor speeds up and starts firing more evenly and the thing is running. Slumping back against the seat, I let the truck run while I think. Sounded like the battery was almost dead. So did I leave a light on somewhere? The headlights are off, so is every other light I can think to check. Maybe the battery is just old and can't sit idle for long before dying or going bad or whatever it is batteries do. Now I'm mad at Daddy all over again for not teaching me more about cars, not that he knew anything himself. The truck is still running, and I turn on the headlights; they work fine, and the instruments light up a little. Not much, it's not that dark in the barn with the sunlight coming through the cracks between the boards, but enough for me to see the gas gauge is close to the E. I need to drive down to the gas station and fill the tank.

The closest station is two miles away and pretty busy most of the time. I try to decide when it would be best to go. I don't want to run into anybody I know and sure as hell don't want to run into Deputy Fife. Our town sits across the river from the county seat and we're not big enough for our own police, so they send a cruiser over a few times a week to loop around the school and the few businesses. Nothing much happens here, and most everybody knows when the policeman,- I try to think of his real name and finally remember that it's Anderson, Jerry Anderson , makes his rounds. I think that today is one of the days he stays on his side of the river, which makes it a good day to get some gas. I put the truck in reverse and start backing and hit the barn door, which I haven't opened.

I put the truck in drive and pull away from the door and get out, hoping I can still open the damn door. It's not damaged, no thanks to my stupidity, and I swing the doors wide and get back in the truck. This time I make it out without running into anything.

After I clear the door, I stop and get out, heading back to the barn. Then I realize that I shouldn't close the barn door; I'll be back in fifteen minutes or so, and this way I can pull right in and get it out of sight quicker. So I leave it, go in the house and get a twenty, and head out on the road.

It's my first time driving anywhere except around the fields. Daddy and I did that early this summer and he made me get out after I almost took out part of the fence around the garden. "Damn fool can't do anything right," is what he said. "Just go on back to the house, back to your Momma." I tighten my grip on the wheel thinking about that, how I went back to the house and into my room and stayed until he came back in and dragged me out, calling me a baby sulking in his crib. I stop the truck before I pull out on the road, trying to calm myself down.

The trip to the station is pretty easy once I get the feel of the truck. It seems enormous, like it takes up almost all the road, and the first time I meet a car, the Jenkins's I think, I almost put the truck in the ditch. When I get to the gas station I pull up to the pump, get out, and realize the gas cap is on the other side, so I have to get back in and turn around. I finally get into the right position, hoping nobody noticed, and go in to the convenience store.

"I'll take fifteen in gas. I'll be in after I fill up to get a couple more things."

The guy behind the counter looks at me a little strange, but nods and takes the twenty. "It shuts off by itself," he says. "Pump two, right?"

I nod and head out, feeling his eyes on me all the way back to the truck. I put fifteen dollars of regular in the tank, hoping that's the right grade, and pull away and park beside the store. When I get out I see the cover to the gas tank open and remember that I didn't put the cap back on. It's sitting on top of the pump, so I run over and grab it, twist it closed and close the cover, and go into the store.

I pass the beer section because I know I would just get laughed at, grab a candy bar and a can of Thunderstorm Soda, and pay at the counter. The guy is still looking at me and I finally say, "Something on your mind?" I know it's a stupid move, I'm trying to stay invisible, but he was starting to piss me off a little.

"Usually see your Daddy in that truck."

Oh shit. I try to just blow it off, but my mouth is really dry all of a sudden.

"Yeah, he's kind of under the weather. Asked me to get a little gas."

"You got a license?"

I laugh. "Hell, no, I don't have a license. I'm just coming down to the store for some gas, not going to Atlanta or anywhere that anybody cares."

He looks at me and then almost smiles. "Yeah, I might've run the roads a little myself back a few years ago. You better get on home before somebody sees you that can't remember what they did when they were your age."

I nod. "That's where I'm headed."

"Tell your daddy to get better. Uncle Frank needs him back in the field soon as he can get there."

"I'll tell him." Now I'm thinking I need to get out of here quick as I can, before he starts asking more questions about Daddy. I back away from the counter and almost knock the next customer down. I don't wait to see if it's anybody I recognize, just head out and jump in the truck. When I turn the key it takes a second and I think I'm in deep trouble, but it catches and then I'm out on the road headed back to the house.

When I get back home I pull into the barn and let the truck run for a few minutes, looking at the gas gauge. Three quarters of a tank. I make a note to come out every other day and start it up, let it run for a few minutes, keep the battery charged. And I wonder what I'm going to do if something really goes wrong with the truck. Not much, I guess.

The candy bar and Thunderstorm Soda make a pretty good lunch, and I catch a nap, make another trip out to the pool, and almost finish the first jar of shine that evening. I'm starting to like this, sipping and watching TV and not thinking about much of anything. I don't stay up much past midnight, thinking I'll try school again tomorrow.

School is feeling more and more like a waste of my time. I stay out of trouble, but I can feel it, the teachers, especially in English class, are going to start paying more attention to me if I slide too far. I never was a great student, but now I'm really awful, and they're going to ask me about that sooner or later. I don't know exactly what to do about that. I never was a star but I was a pretty good student; funny how that's working against me now. I'd pick a fight or bring some shine to school or something that would get me kicked out but then they'd want to talk to Momma and Daddy, and I can't call attention to that.

Maybe what I need to do is come up with some kind of story about Daddy so when people ask I'll have something ready. I've been blindsided a couple of times now already and I don't like that.

I take today off from school, still a great feeling to just decide that, and decide to take a little inventory. Still nothing from Momma and Hannah, and I don't want to call them until I come up with something about Daddy that makes sense and is too much trouble to check out. For now I need to see what I've got.

Money — I've got the two hundred behind the canned tomatoes, the two hundred in my underwear drawer, and a hundred and sixty-two in my pocket.

Food — refrigerator's got baloney, cheese, drinks, something in the vegetable drawer that looks slimy. Canned soup and tomatoes and beans and one more jar of that salsa that Hannah talked Momma into on the shelf in the cabinet. A box of elbow macaroni.

Shine — three full jars and one about one-fourth full.

Gas — three quarters of a tank in the truck.

Seems like a lot to me.

My trips to the pool are the best part of the day; I'm going up almost every day now, and I'm changing up the time of day, since I don't have anybody setting the schedule for me. I know I've got to figure out what to do when people ask about Daddy, but seems like it would dirty the place to think about it up there, so I sit down to try to figure something out before I go up there today.

He's been gone way over a week now, and nobody has asked about him, unless you count the guy at the gas station. So that's good, not many people miss him. I know I don't. For just a flicker of time I'm ashamed of that, since he was my Daddy and all, but I get over that pretty quick. All I have to do is think about having to clean up his mess and the shame is gone.

Nobody's asked me about Momma, and I think that's weird until I remember that nobody's asked about Hannah either, and I've been to school a few times since they left. I guess Momma must've told the school she was taking Hannah with her and I would be staying here and finishing out the school year with Daddy. It would help to know if she did talk to the school and what kind of lie she made up if that was the case. I don't want to call and ask her until I figure out what to say about Daddy.

So what can I say? I could say he found work somewhere out of town, but that doesn't explain the truck. It would explain most everything else, though, so I give that some more thought. I know he hung out with a bunch of those guys he worked the fields with, even though he talked about them behind their back. He did that with everybody except me, and he never waited until my back was turned to talk his trash about me. Did it right to my face. Now I'm mad all over again and I have to let that go away so I can think.

The leaving for work somewhere else kind of makes sense, so I see if it needs any more work before I try it out on somebody. There's the truck. That's the big problem. I could say it broke down and he got pissed off and told me he was going to catch a ride to the next place they were picking. He'd already be mad because of Momma and Hannah, so that works too.

I'll tell people, if anybody asks, that he got mad and left when the truck wouldn't start. No, that won't work because I drove it to the gas station. Damn fool thing to do. Maybe the transmission started slipping and he got mad about that and just left it. That makes sense; everybody that knew Daddy knew about his temper. I remember one time in the middle of town he got mad at the truck and started beating on the hood. Had quite a crowd before he finally wore down, so if anybody remembered that, him getting mad at the truck would make sense.

Yeah, that works. He came home mad about the truck transmission and then got the note from Momma, and that really sent him over the edge, he stormed out and I haven't seen him since. Okay.

I feel like I need to check on the grave. When I get to the little field the ground has settled even more, that part's barely noticeable, but the kudzu kind of stands out out there in the middle of the field with no more kudzu anywhere around it, but maybe that's because I'm looking for it. It's growing, couple of new shoots and the leaves look good, so I think that a couple more weeks and it won't stand out so much. The rest of the grass in the field is getting higher and that helps too. We had sold what few animals we had a couple of years ago and what's growing there isn't worth baling, so I'm not worried about that.

I go back into the house and take a look in Momma's room. Still pretty much of a mess, and I start to clean it up when I realize that it's kind of evidence about my story about them being mad at each other. Maybe I should leave it alone. I think I will leave it alone.

Hannah's room I also decide to leave alone and I go on down to my room. Frankie's side is still just the way Momma insisted that it stay, like he was coming back anytime, and it gets me thinking.

How many lies did Momma tell herself and try to keep secret from everybody? That Frankie wasn't dead? That Daddy would turn out to be a good husband if she just worked at it hard enough?

Then I wonder what kind of lies she told herself about me.

I don't like thinking about this stuff, so I go in and turn on the TV. I mix some shine with a little Thunderstorm Soda, sit down in front of the TV, and start flipping channels. There's nothing on, as usual, but I find a movie I haven't seen yet and settle in for the evening.

There's a knock on the door.

Chapter Eight

I panic for a minute and then try to get myself together; whoever it is is at the front door, which we never use. We always use the kitchen door. So this is somebody I don't know. I take a quick peek out the side window and see a silver Honda sitting in the yard. Don't know the car. For a second I consider pretending I'm not home, but I had the TV on pretty loud, so that probably won't work. I go to the front door and open it a crack.

"Yeah?"

"Mr. Everett?"

I try not to breathe on the guy. "No, one more house up."

"Thanks."

I open the door a little farther. The man is in a suit and has a briefcase.

"Everything okay?"

He turns back. "Just some business with Mr. Everett. Are you a friend?"

I nod. "Lived here for years."

He sighs. "You might want to look in on him later on."

Turning back, he goes to his car, gets in, and backs out into the road. As he drives up the road I wonder what is going on with old man Everett. Maybe I'll look in on him tomorrow.

The next morning is halfway gone before I remember that I was going to check on the old man. I get on my bike and ride up to his house; the place looks like it usually does, like nobody lives there.

When I get up on the porch I see that the front door is open. I've never seen that before, and I stop while I try to figure out what to do. Finally I open the screen door and knock on the glass.

"Mr. Everett? It's Boone from down the hill. Everything okay?"

I hear something I can't make out. Pushing the door farther open, I try again.

"Mr. Everett? Are you okay?"

It shocks me when the music starts. It's low and mournful, like, and doesn't sound like a radio. Too many mistakes, and the song starts and stops over and over. I take a step inside the front room, the first time I've been in his house. Maybe the first time anybody in this town has been in his house.

The music is louder now, and sounds like it's right in front of me. It's really gloomy in here, no lights that I can see, and the windows all have heavy curtains that cover most of every window. I take another step. It sounds like fiddle music; does old man Everett play the fiddle?

The song stops and starts up again, and this time I hear a voice. It's his, and it sounds like he's having to force the words out. I listen for a minute and recognize the song. Momma used to take us to church and tried to get Daddy to go, and didn't give up until after Frankie died. But I remember the old hymns, the four part harmonies, and this was one they played and sang every other week.

"Just a closer walk with theeeee . . . . granted Jesus is my pleeeaaaa . . . . ." then the voice, which is definitely old man Everett's, sounding like a man weeping and singing at the same time, gives way to the fiddle and it stumbles through part of the song and then there's a crash and the sound of a man crying, weeping. I take another step and I'm at a wide doorway to my left and I'm looking into an old parlor, looks like one of those old movies from the classic movie channel, all dark wood and a thick rug on the floor and a mantel with what looks like a hundred pictures on it and old man Everett sitting on a footstool with his head in his hands and a fiddle at his feet.

I step on into the room and it's a minute before he notices me.

He just stares at me for a few seconds and then puts his head back down. He's staring at the fiddle, which looks like it's still in one piece.

"Mr. Everett, a guy stopped by my house yesterday looking for you and said I should check on you. Did something happen? Can I do something?"

I've never tried to comfort anybody outside my family before. It feels weird, like I'm intruding. I guess I am intruding, in his house for the first time, and him sitting in front of me all broken and sad. I don't know what else to say, so I just stand there feeling foolish.

We stay that way for four minutes; I know because up on the mantel there's a clock with a loud tick and I noticed the time when I came in. After the four minutes, I decide that I should leave and now I don't know whether or not to say goodbye, I'll come back later, hope you feel better. I don't know what has happened to make him so sad and so I don't know what to say. I decide on nothing and start to turn when he looks up at me.

"What did you say?"

I'm confused for a minute and then realize that he's asking about what I said four minutes ago.

"I said that a guy stopped by yesterday looking for you and said I should check on you."

"Did he say anything else?"

"No, sir, nothing else."

"Good. Nobody's damn business. Not your business either. Damn nosy neighbors."

I wince a little at that; it sounds like something Daddy might say. Then I remind myself that he's not Daddy and that Daddy would say that about any little thing. Mr. Everett is really upset about something. I wonder it somebody in his family is dead, but I can't think how to ask, and besides, he's kind of told me to get out just now. So I start to turn again.

"You sure he didn't say anything else?"

His voice is still thin, but easier to hear without a door between us. I take a chance and step closer.

"Yes, sir, I'm sure. Can I get you anything or do something for you? You look really sad."

He doesn't say anything for what seems like another four minutes, but was probably more like ten seconds. Then, "You just go on home now."

I didn't move.

"You hear me? Go on back down the hill to your old drunk daddy and leave me alone!"

His voice is not loud, but maybe as loud as he can make it. He starts to get up.

I put my hands out in front of me like I was going to push him back down, but I back up instead and say, "I'm going, going right now."

When I get out on the porch I close the door and the screen and head on back home.

Two days later I'm back on his front porch. I'm not sure why I'm there, just can't get the old guy out of my mind. Still no word from Momma or Hannah, nobody seems much interested in me which I think is just fine, but it gives me time to think about stuff. And what I'm thinking is that I should go back and check on Mr. Everett.

So here I am, getting ready to knock on his door, when it opens a crack and I see him looking out at me.

"Thought I told you to go on home."

"You did, Mr. Everett, and that's just what I did. That was day before yesterday and I just thought I'd come back and look in on you again, if that's all right with you."

He closes the door.

Stubborn old fart, I think to myself as I'm going back down the steps. You don't have to worry about me coming back and bothering you again.

Another week goes by with no word from Momma or Hannah, and I'm back and forth between being mad at them and feeling sorry for myself. Then I realize that what I have not done since all this started is check the mailbox.

It's full to overflowing, but I can tell before I even get back to the house that a lot of it is trash. I sit down and start sorting; everything is going into the throwaway pile and then I run across two I set aside.

85

One is the electric bill; I knew that was coming sooner or later and I was dreading opening that one, and the other one is addressed to me in Momma's handwriting. I open the electric bill first; $68.45. Damn. I think I'm screwed until I remember that there were four of us in here for a lot of that. Still need to be careful.

Before opening Momma's letter, I get a glass and pour a little shine into it and add a little ice. That finishes off the first jar, but I'll think about that later. I take a drink and tear the envelope.

There's money in here, folded inside a two-page letter. Fifty dollars.

The letter reads:

Dear Son,

I am sending you this money because I know your Daddy never ever checks the mail. I hope you remember to.

That night, the night I called Claire, was the worst. Your Daddy has been drunk and mean before, but I just couldn't take it anymore. I felt like a coward leaving the two of you, but I was so scared. Still am.

When I talked to Hannah and told her that Claire would pick her up from school, it broke my heart that you weren't there for me to talk to. I wanted to tell you instead of writing it all down, but it's been too long now and I need to let you know what I've decided.

I can't come back. Not ever. Your daddy has done some things, you know that, but he's done some things you don't know about and I can't tell you because I'm too ashamed, I can't even think about them without crying, and I need to finish this letter. I had to leave to get away from all that because he wasn't going to stop, not ever. And I had to get Hannah out of there before she got older and he (she had something here and scratched it out, almost tore a hole in the paper, I can't make out what it was) noticed her. She's just a little girl, just seven years old. I had to get her out of there.

It's different with you. You're almost a man, you can leave soon and get away from him. The only thing he'll do to you is give you a beating, and you're getting so big that won't last much longer. Don't let him turn you mean like him, Boone, don't let him do that to you. He's ruined me, I had to get out to save Hannah, and it tore me apart not to take you with us.

You stay in school, you hear me? You stay in school and get that diploma and then get out of there. Leave him to himself. He was a good man once, back when he was courting me, he was so good-looking and used to get me things and tell me how pretty I was, but all that's gone now, I don't think he'll change back, he's too far down that road. You can't turn out like him, there's too much good in you, I know that, I've seen it.

I'll send more money when I can. Claire is going to help me get a job and she says I can stay with them as long as I need to. I love you and hope to see you someday. Don't tell your daddy about this or the money and maybe you should burn this letter or take it to school and throw it away. The envelope too. All of it. I don't think he remembers where Claire lives but I can't take a chance on that.

I love you,
Momma

I read it through two or three times, and then toss it on the table. I feel like I'm about to cry and I feel like I'm about to tear something up and I don't know which way to go. I'm trembling, sitting there, and I'm thinking how could you leave me Momma and then maybe I should call her and tell her about Daddy and then no I can't do that she'll come back down here and make me dig him up so she can bury him proper or maybe so she can see for herself he's dead and then I'm looking around the room and I see stuff that makes me think of Momma everywhere I look and then I'm tearing stuff off the walls and ripping drawers open and shouting at the ceiling and then I'm on the floor crying, crying.

It takes me a while to stop and then I get up and look around the room. It's a mess. It looks just like it did that night when Daddy tore it up, when he hit Momma, the night just before she left and I know I've got some of Daddy in me and it scares me, scares me to death. I don't want that part but I look around the room and I know it's in there. It's in there if I get pushed hard enough.

Right then I understand Daddy a little better than I have in a long time, maybe ever. He got walked on and pushed around out there, on his job, in the town, and he had to push back, and he couldn't push them, and so we were it. What we did didn't have to be big, or even real, it was just all inside him and it had to come out and it came out all over us.

Chapter Nine

I get that. And maybe I still hate him but not quite as much as before.

"The kitchen won't clean itself," I say to the empty living room. Somehow I am on the couch, don't remember how that happened, and I think it's time for me to get up and clean up my own mess. Momma's not here to do it, Daddy's in the ground out back, so if it's going to get clean, it's me. So I get out the jar of shine that I've been drinking on since the first jar ran out and take a look. Still quite a bit, but I'm going to have to do something about that, only two jars after this one and I'm out. I don't want to be out. I pour a little and add a little ice and start in on the kitchen.

I'm just finishing the kitchen when there's a knock on the door. The front door again. I start to head into the living room to open it and remember that jar of shine sitting on the kitchen counter. I put it with the others in the cabinet and go to the door and open it a crack.

It's Deputy Fife.

"Can I help you?" I say around a really dry mouth, hoping I don't smell like shine.

"Need to ask you a couple of questions."

I open the door and step out beside him before he can go inside. It's crowded up there, so I go down into the yard and turn to face him. "About what?"

"About your daddy. His field boss hasn't seen him in a couple of weeks and he's hurting for workers. Asked me to find out if he's planning to come back or not. I gotta tell you, Boone, he's pretty pissed at your old man for just walking out on him like that. Your daddy home? He's really the one I need to talk to. Although I would like to know why you're not in school," he looks at me suspiciously.

Okay, here goes, I say to myself. "I don't know where he is, to tell you the truth. He came in all mad a couple of weeks ago, something about some guy on the job said something about his hand, you know, the one he got hurt," I look at him and he nods, everybody knows about Daddy's hand, "and how he wasn't going to put up with that and then he started to take off in the truck and the transmission started slipping and he got really mad, mad as I've ever seen him."

The deputy is just standing there, looking at me. So I keep going.

"So he comes back in the house, slamming doors and scaring everybody, and says he's outta here, there's more work the next county over. He takes off down the road, walking real fast, and I haven't seen him since."

I stop and take a breath and look at the deputy. He's nodding, and I'm thinking this might work.

"Your daddy's got a temper, I know that."

"Yes sir." I don't think I should say any more, so I just wait.

"So can I talk to your Momma?"

"She went up to visit her sister Claire up in Bristol for a few days. She was real upset when he didn't come back. Want me to have her call you when she gets back in town?"

He sighs. "Just if she knows any more than you, I guess. I'll tell them I came out and asked and they better not count on him. You get yourself back in school, you hear?"

"Yes sir."

He heads back to his car and turns it around and is gone.

My legs just about buckle under me, and I head back to the house and into the kitchen. I don't care if I'm running low, I pour another drink, strong this time, and go sit on the couch.

He bought it, I'm pretty sure. Word is about him that he doesn't work any harder than he has to, and this thing about Daddy skipping out on work probably just irritated him. Somebody noticed that he doesn't do anything when he comes over here besides drive around and drink coffee at the diner, and decided to give him something to do. I wonder if he'll write up a report or anything or just forget about it. I'm counting on him just forgetting about it.

The next day I realize it's been over a week since I was at old man Everett's house. I haven't seen any traffic in or out except the Thompson's trucks, nobody going to the Everett place, and I'm thinking I should go by and see if he's okay. Hard to know what to do there; I don't know anything about why the guy came to see him or why the old man was so upset, so I don't know what to ask about. I'll go up there the next day, I decide. Today I'm going up to the pool; it's been a few days and I miss it, plus it's still hot enough to make it feel really good under the trees.

When I get there it's just like I left it the last time, all quiet and green and beautiful. The kind of place to bring a girl, and for some reason Nancy comes to mind. I've stayed away from her ever since that scene in the cafeteria and haven't thought about her at all, so why now? I shrug it off and settle back on the rocks.

After a while I decide to go walking around, something I don't do up here. Never felt like I needed anything else besides the pool, but for some reason I want to find out what else is here. I'm still on our land, so I just strike out across the woods, breaking trail as I go.

Until I come across a faint trail about fifty yards from the pool. I stand there and stare down at it. There shouldn't be anything else here; nobody should be snooping around back in these woods. I look up and down the trail, what little bit I can see, trying to decide which way to follow it. No reason to pick one over the other, so I turn away from the house and start picking my way along.

It's a hard trail to follow, a lot like the one to my pool. Three or four times I almost lose it, but find it again and keep going. I'm getting close to our property line, I think, but I'm not sure. Never been out in this part of the woods before.

It looks like the woods thin out up ahead, and I slow down, paranoid for no reason. I'm still on our land, got every right to be here. Still I'm extra careful as more light comes in and there's definitely a clearing ahead of me.

I come to the edge of the clearing and can barely keep from laughing out loud. I've seen pictures of stills in the history books, and they were rusty, misshapen contraptions that looked like a good strong breeze would blow them over. This one looks a lot like those pictures, so I figure it must be something Daddy put together. Like everything else, he did a half-ass job of it, and I step up to it expecting it to fall apart any second.

It's got all the parts, and Daddy even used a coil instead of an old radiator for the condenser. I've heard that using one of them is how some of the heavier drinkers got lead poisoning. It looks like it has been used this season, but not tended for a little while, which makes sense, Daddy being in the ground and all.

Momma used to shake her head about Daddy using up all the money he made out in the fields buying liquor. Guess he had at least one secret from her. Nobody makes their own anymore; everybody's growing pot or cooking meth; Daddy liked the old ways, I guess.

Walking around the clearing, I can see a pipe running through the woods toward the creek. There's a little pile of wood close to the pit, and half a dozen jars on a flat rock off to the side. Five of them look full.

This is better than a will, I think to myself, picking up one of the jars and unscrewing the lid. I take a sip, then a full drink. Same stuff I've got at home.

There's an old nail barrel up on a platform built of rocks, and I look at that next. It's heavy, and when I pull the top off the smell almost knocks me on my ass. There must be six or eight gallons in here, fermenting from the smell of it, ready to do something with. Trouble is, I don't know what to do with it. If I tried to get this thing running again I'd probably set the woods on fire or call the law down on me. I take a couple of jars and head back down the trail which, sure enough, comes out of the woods across the burying ground from the barn. I step around Daddy's grave, almost invisible now, and head straight for the kitchen.

I put the two jars in the cabinet with the ones I found out in the barn; that gives me five altogether, enough to last for a while, plus there are some still up in the clearing. I wonder who I can ask about running that thing. It's a real old setup, I'm sure they do it a lot fancier now, and the guys I know from school wouldn't know how, even if I thought I could trust them, which I don't. I'll figure this all out tomorrow or the next day, I decide. Right now I need some food, and I think I'll have a drink to celebrate. I go to the refrigerator and look inside.

There's only one two liter left. I'm going to need some more.

I bring the rest of the jars down the next day, and set them on the kitchen table along with all the others. Eight full jars of shine. Plus whatever's in that nail keg, six or eight gallons. How much would that make after I do whatever it is I am supposed to do with it? Two, maybe three more gallons? If I learn how to do this, I could make some money. The more I think about this idea, the better I like it.

First thing I need to do is find out how to run a still. We never got a computer, Daddy said it was a waste of money and Momma never argued about that stuff. They said we could use the library's computers, so that's what Hannah and I have been doing for school and stuff. I don't want to do that, though, there's only four computers down there and it's kind of public. That librarian's always looking over folk's shoulders, even though I don't think she's supposed to. Last thing I need is to try to have to explain that.

Then I think of old man Everett.

Chapter Ten

As soon as I think of him I feel guilty. I haven't been up to check on him for a while now, and he was in kind of bad shape the last time I was there. He's got nobody, just like me, and I'm his closest neighbor. I should be looking in on him.

Wonder if he likes shine.

There's some little jars that Momma used to put up whatever pickles or tomatoes or whatever wouldn't fit into the regular size jars when she was canning. I look around and find one, unscrew the lid, and pour it about half full. No sense giving away too much until I find out about this.

The whole idea makes me nervous. I don't really know much about the old guy. The name on the mailbox is G. Everett, he lives by himself, he's older than anybody else I know, he has a lot of tools, he plays the fiddle, and something bad happened not too long ago. I don't even know what the something bad was, but it sure hit him hard.

So I don't know if he even likes shine or, if he does, if he knows how a still works. He might be one of those Bible-thumping Baptists that'll call down the wrath of God and all the good people of the town on me. Somehow I don't see that, but the fact is I don't know. If he does know how one works, and he doesn't turn me in to the church or the police, then I might be able to at least use what's in that keg instead of having to pour it out on the ground. The thought of doing that makes me a little sick, wasting all that shine. I decide then and there that I'm going to take a chance on this. I just have to figure out how to bring it up. Fact is, I've never taken him anything, always gone up there to get something, except for that last time. He was acting like somebody died; maybe I should be taking food instead of shine to him.

Momma used to bake pies, I remember. She made the best peach pie you ever put in your mouth, and, when somebody died, that's what she would make. When I think about people dying, I think about how the house would smell like peach pie cooking. That feels weird how those two things go together in my head. But I don't know how to make a pie, peach or apple or cherry or any other kind, so I can't do what Momma did. I wish she was here so she could do that for old man Everett.

She'd roll out the dough and always have some little bits left over to bake with the pie for Hannah and me and Frankie when he was still alive. What we wanted, though, was a big slice of pie right out of the oven. One time she made one when nobody had died, just for the family, and she got a little box of vanilla ice cream and we had it right out of the oven with a spoonful of that ice cream on top. It was heaven right there in our kitchen.

Then Daddy came home all drunk and mad and yelling about wasting money on pies and all the good feelings just ran right out of the kitchen and so did us kids and that night Daddy was really mean to Momma, shouting at her and calling her names and then he took the rest of the pie and threw it out in the yard. I really hated him that night.

Momma didn't bake pies for us after that, and pretty much stopped baking them for anybody else. I guess she didn't want to give Daddy another reason to yell at her and throw things around. He had enough reasons, sometimes we never figured out what they were.

I shake my head, hard, and try to stop thinking about pies and all that, I'm close to crying again and that makes me mad at myself. I try to start thinking about what I'm going to say to old man Everett when I go up there, and how I'm going to get him to help me if he knows how to work a still.

When I get to his house it looks different, somehow, and I can't figure it out until I get to the front door and it's a different color and I look around and notice that the front porch has been painted. Same color, which is why I didn't notice right off, but the color's all even and there aren't any leaves or sticks or anything on the porch. I hesitate for a minute and then knock on the door. I hear footsteps almost immediately, but they don't sound like old man Everett's. The door opens.

The woman standing there looks kind of like him, mostly in the eyes, and she looks at me without saying anything for a minute and then says, "Is your name Boone?"

"Yes, ma'am." I'm a little nervous, with that jar of shine in my backpack, but I answer her and then just wait.

"Pop's been asking about you. I think you're the only company he's had up here in years. Won't you come in?"

Pop, I think. Well, that's why she looks like him. I step into the house and she closes the door.

"Want to hang that pack up somewhere or let me set it down for you?"

I tighten my grip on the strap. "No, that's all right, I can't stay. I just came to check on him. The last time I was here he was awful sad."

Her face clouds. "I told them not to tell him about that until I could be here to stay with him for a few days. Damn lawyers."

"Yes, ma'am." I have no idea what she was talking about.

"Did Pop tell you what happened?"

I shake my head.

"My brother was killed in an accident. He was on vacation in Europe and a ferry went down, no survivors. I should have been here when they told him his son was gone."

"Yes, ma'am."

"He took it hard, said you came up and he ran you off. He's sorry about that."

"You tell him not to worry about that, ma'am. He didn't cuss me or anything like that. Just wanted to be left alone. Tell him not to worry."

She smiles, a thin little smile, but her eyes were sad like his were last time I saw him.

"I'll tell him, unless you want to tell him yourself. He's just back in the kitchen."

"No, that's okay, I don't want to bother." What I want is to get out of there and go back home.

"You sure? I'm baking a pie. You're welcome to stay and have a piece."

Now I really want to get out of here. I start backing toward the door.

"No, thank you, I really need to get back home."

She looks at me kind of strange. By then I'm back at the door and I'm feeling for the knob. I finally give up and turn around so I can see what I'm looking for. I turn the handle and pull the door open.

"Wait a minute, Boone."

I'm already out on the porch, but I stop and turn back around to face her.

"My husband's coming by later on today to pick me up. We live up in Cleveland now. Will you look in on Pop a couple of times a week after I go back home?"

I nod and step off the porch.

She follows me down into the yard and puts a hand on my shoulder.

I turn again; she's right in front of me now, looking up at me.

"Listen, Boone, I know he's not the friendly sort. Likes being by himself. He's been that way long as I can remember. He might not seem like he cares whether you come by or not, but it would make me feel better. Do you live real close?"

I point toward the house.

"You can't see it during the summer, but it's right down there. Pretty soon, when the leaves drop, it'll be easy to see."

"I'll stop by there on the way out later today and give you my phone number and some money in case he needs anything." She looks me up and down. "Too bad you're too young to buy beer. Pop likes a drink every now and then."

I don't say anything to that, but inside I'm smiling. So old man Everett likes a drink every now and then? I'm glad to know that.

"Anyway," she says, "We'll stop by on the way out. It'll be close to dark."

I say that would be fine and she goes in and I go back home.

When they stop by she doesn't come to the door; it's this guy I guess is her husband. He hands me a piece of paper with a phone number on it and four twenties. He looks at me like he's mad at me about something.

"Here's our number and some money. You be sure and spend that on Pop, you hear?"

I feel like throwing the money right back in his stupid face.

"Yeah," I say.

He goes back to his car and they leave.

I go back in the house, slamming the door shut.

What the hell was that? She seemed like a nice person, and now this asshole comes onto my property treating me like I'm a piece of dog shit he scraped off his shoe. I'm halfway down the hall to the closet when I realize they're already gone, too late to do anything.

I put the note and the twenties on the kitchen counter and open the refrigerator. I really need to go to the store, I say to myself. I ran out of baloney again and the cheese is gone. Wonder how one of those frozen pizzas would taste?

The store is not so far I can't make it easy on the bicycle, but I'm part way out the door when I notice the truck keys hanging on the nail next to the door. Well, why the hell not?

I've been going out every three or four days and starting it up, letting it run a few minutes, but I haven't had it out on the road since filling it up with gas. It's here, I think to myself, nobody else is going to use it. I grab the keys and head for the barn.

The truck starts right up, and I back out of the barn and turn around in the yard. It's close to dark, and I wonder if I need headlights. Better not draw attention to myself, I think, and find the switch on the dash, turn them on, and head for the grocery store.

It takes long enough to get the pizzas, one for now and one for later, a couple of two liter bottles of Thunderstorm Soda, and a few other things that it's close to full night when I get out of the store. I turn on the headlights and head back to the house.

About halfway home I feel like I'm being followed. This makes me really nervous, and I slow down and make sure I use the signals and all that, and make it back to the house without running any stop signs or making any other mistakes. At least that's what I think.

The car that's been right behind me pulls into the yard and I see it's the deputy. Shit, I think, what'll I do now?

I get out with my bag of groceries and he gets out and comes up to me.

"Evening, Boone."

"How ya doin', Deputy?"

I'm trying to stay calm and pretend like everything's okay.

"Do you know why I followed you into your yard, Boone?"

"No, sir, I don't."

"Well," he says, "I figure you might have forgotten to take your license with you to the store and I didn't want to have to write you up."

I take a deep breath.

"You have a taillight out. Need to get that fixed. I will pull you over the next time." He looks at me. "Pizza tonight?"

I nod.

"Heard anything from your daddy?"

I shake my head no.

He shakes his head. "Sorry to hear that." He looks at me hard for a second or two. "How about your momma?"

"She's still visiting her sister."

There is a long silence, both of us looking at the ground. I'm about to say that I need to get these pizzas in the freezer when he looks up.

"Well, I need to make my rounds. You take care now."

"I will."

He drives off and I go into the kitchen and collapse into a chair.

Why is he being nice to me? Everything I've heard about this guy is that he's a lazy little shit. I don't know what to do with this. Maybe he wants something, but for the life of me I can't think what that might be. Does he know about the still? Is he waiting for me to mess up, lead him to it, something like that?

I can't figure it out, so I look at the instructions to find out how to make the pizza.

Chapter Eleven

It turns out pretty good, and I finish almost all of it and watch TV until I fall asleep on the couch. I haven't bothered with my bed in a long time.

The next morning I decide to go to school; it's been a while and I need to show up every now and then. Not much going on, same old stuff, Curt is really into his new group of buddies, and I'm even more outside than I used to be. Funny that it doesn't bother me as much now.

I eat quick and get out of the cafeteria so I can have some time outside before my next class. I have less patience with sitting in a desk now, and I don't know how many more times I can make myself go.

I'm sitting on a bench in the grassy area inside the bus turnaround, half asleep in the afternoon sun, when a noise wakes me. Nancy sits down beside me.

"Haven't seen you around lately, Boone."

I'm trying to wake up; I really was close to dozing off. "No, guess not."

"You're going to end up failing all your classes, you know. You'll have to take them again next year."

I shrug.

She doesn't say anything for a few minutes and I'm dropping off again when she says, "You want to come over tonight so I can help you get caught up? I'm pretty good at history, and a lot has happened since you were there."

I shake my head. "Truck's got a busted taillight. Deputy Fife already pulled me over once and let me off with a warning. Better not push it. He might tase me."

She laughed. "We wouldn't want that, I guess."

There was another long silence and then she said, "I better get back inside. I've got a test next period."

She gets up and starts to leave. I try to think of something to say and finally say, "I'll try to get a new bulb for the truck."

She looks back at me. "That's good. Wouldn't want anybody to hit you in the ass."

I laugh out loud without thinking about it.

"See you around, Nancy."

"See you, Boone."

I watch her go, thinking she looks pretty good from behind. Wonder what she'd look like without those glasses on? I stand up and try to decide whether or not to bother with the afternoon classes. I'm already listed as present, and I can cut across the

Jenkins and Thompson farms and get home pretty quick.

It's not a hard decision, and I head off toward the Jenkins place. They've got about 400 acres, so I'm not worried about running into anybody. The Thompson place is even bigger, but when I get to the fence and start to cross into their land I can't help but remember Daddy telling me to stay off their property, how they didn't like people snooping around.

I'm standing there trying to decide what to do when I hear a four-wheeler headed my way. It's coming at me over Thompson land, from one of their barns I can see just over the first hill. I stand there, knowing that I'm caught out in the open. I'm not on their land, but they could still be assholes about it if they wanted to. They're one of the big farms around here.

It's Mrs. Thompson, which surprises me. I never would have expected to see her out here, much less on a four-wheeler. She always struck me as the Cadillac type.

She pulls up and kills the engine.

"Boone, isn't it?"

"Yes, Mrs. Thompson." I start to say something else and then think the best thing I can do is keep quiet.

She squints at me. "School let out early today?"

"No, ma'am, I just thought . . ."

"Just thought you'd skip a class or two?" She shakes her head, but there's a little smile, barely there. "I practically had to tie my oldest to the desk to get him through his senior year. You a senior, Boone?"

"Junior."

She waggles a finger at me. "Too soon to be getting into this habit. You headed home?"

I nod.

"I don't usually like people on my land that have no business there, but since you're this close, you go on ahead. Just don't make a habit of it, hear?"

"Thanks." I don't know what else to say, so I climb over the fence and land right in front of the four-wheeler.

"Get moving before I change my mind."

"Yes ma'am. Thank you, Mrs. Thompson."

She waves a hand. "Word is your daddy ran off and left you all. I don't plan to add to your troubles. Just don't take advantage."

"I won't."

She waits until I'm out of the way and then starts it up and guns it, slides around until she's pointing back to the barn, and takes off, bouncing through the rough field like a teenager.

I watch her go, shaking my head. Never would have figured that.

It's an easy walk to the property line, and I'm close to my pool. I decide not to go there, not just yet. Maybe go home, have a nap, see if I feel like it later. I need to check on old man Everett, and make up my mind to do that tomorrow. For now I just want to relax. Funny how half a day of school can take it out of you if you're out of the habit of going.

The next afternoon I put the little jar of shine in my backpack again and head up to Mr. Everett's house. Partly I'm going up there because his daughter asked me to, partly because I'm hoping he knows how to run a still, and partly to have somebody to talk to. I've been by myself a lot lately, and I usually like that, but not quite this much.

When I knock on the front door, I hear footsteps almost immediately. The door opens a crack and old man Everett peeks out.

"Hi, Mr. Everett. I'm Boone from — "

"I know who you are. My daughter said you came up here but you wouldn't come in and say hello. Damned impolite."

I just stand there, surprised into silence. He keeps looking at me through the crack.

I finally say, "Your daughter asked me to look in on you from time to time."

"Well, here I am."

This is awkward, I don't know what to do next, stay or go or what. I take a deep breath and say, "May I come in?"

He doesn't answer, just steps away from the door and opens it a little farther. I take that as a yes and open the screen door again, step through, and close the door behind me.

He's halfway down the hall. He turns to look at me. "Coming?"

I nod and follow him, into a part of the house I've never seen.

The room we enter is as full of light as the living room where I saw Mr. Everett last was empty of it. Here there are windows on two walls, no curtains, and what furniture there is, which isn't much, is functional, handmade, and really beautiful to look at. He sits in a chair that looks like it was made for him, which I'm guessing it was, and points to another one close by.

When I sit down, the backpack makes a clinking noise when I put it on the floor.

Mr. Everett cocks his head. "What's in the bag, kid?"

Might as well see what happens. I pull the jar out of the backpack and hand it to him. "Your daughter said you might like a beer every now and then and I'm too young to buy beer, so I thought I'd bring you this."

He looks at me, and I look back. He unscrews the lid and takes a quick sniff, then a sip, then a drink.

Then he leans back in his chair, eyes closed, and says, "Ahhhhh. . . ."

Straightening back up, he offers me the jar. I take a drink, a small one since I'm still getting used to drinking it straight, and hand it back to him.

Mr. Everett has another drink, a good long one this time, and sets the jar down on the end table beside him. He gets up and says, "I'll be right back," and goes out of the room.

He's back in a couple of minutes with some cheese and crackers. He hands me a few crackers and a hunk of cheese and says, "Never on an empty stomach."

"Thanks."

We eat and drink in silence, passing the jar back and forth, until it's almost empty and all the food is gone.

"Okay," Mr. Everett says, leaning back. His voice seems stronger, but I'm not sure that it is. The room is swaying a little.

"Okay," he says again. "Where did you get that?"

"In the barn," I say. "Daddy had some hidden in one of the stalls."

"He's going to be really mad when he finds out you've been stealing his shine."

"He's gone."

Mr. Everett looks at me hard. "What do you mean by that?"

"I mean for, like, two or three weeks. He and Momma had a big fight. She's gone too."

He seems to need some time to think about this. The room is very quiet, so quiet I can hear the clock in the front room ticking. Eventually he says, "When are they coming back?"

"They're not. Daddy stormed off, said he'd find work somewhere else. Left his truck and everything. Momma sent me a letter a few days ago. She's got Hannah with her and they're not coming back."

Mr. Everett shakes his head. "What about the other one, don't you have a brother, what is his name?"

"Frankie's dead, Mr. Everett. Over a year now."

He looks down at the floor. "Sorry. I had heard that, just forgot for a second."

There's a long silence after that. Mr. Everett takes another drink, then puts the lid back on and screws it on tight.

"Almost as good as the stuff I make," he says, so low I can barely hear him.

I can hardly believe my luck. Did he really say that? What do I say now?

"So, you used to make this stuff?"

He ignores the question. "Where did you say you got this?"

He knows about the still. I can tell he knows about it. And it just makes sense, it's out his back door and through the woods for a little over a hundred yards, mostly on Thompson land, but then across the creek and onto our land and it's right there. He knows about it. Hell, it might be his, set up on somebody else's land so he can say he doesn't know anything about it.

"In our barn."

"You sure about that?" He doesn't sound mad, just curious.

I'm really not sure what to do and I'm thinking those last couple of sips might not have been such a good idea. Oh, well, I'm this far in. He knows enough to get me in real trouble, although I don't get that feel from him at all. Here goes.

"Yeah, I'm sure, but up in our woods, close to the line with the Thompson land, I found a still that looks like you could use it if you knew how."

He grins. First time I've seen a smile on his face. It makes him look a lot younger and a lot more dangerous all at the same time. It's not a ha-ha kind of grin, more a gotcha kind. I swallow hard.

"Don't you go messing around with that unless you know what you're doing, Boone. You'll get yourself blown up."

I nod because I can't think of what else to do. I want to say the right thing here, get him to help me out, but I can't seem to put three thoughts together without losing track of them. Mr. Everett notices that.

"You also need to learn how to hold your liquor if you're going to sit down with a man and sip shine with him."

I nod again.

"You ever look under the lid on those jars of shine you've got at home?"

This time I shake my head and the room wiggles a little bit after I stop.

"You should."

"Okay." I take a couple of deep breaths and lean forward. He puts up a hand.

"I appreciate the visit, Boone, and this little taste of shine. You come back anytime, anytime at all. Right now I want some time to myself."

I stand up. "Yes, sir. Thanks."

He points down the hall. "You remember how to get home, Boone?"

"Yes, sir, I do. I'll come back up and check on you soon. You need anything from the store when I come?"

The old man shakes his head, slow, and I can see he's done with company right now. I need to get on out of here. I never even asked him about what he was so sad about the last time I was up here, I realize, but now doesn't seem like the right time.

"Well, if you think of anything, your daughter left me some money for store — "

His back is to me but I can see him get all tense and his neck is getting a little red. I start down the hall; I need to get out of here before I say something else stupid. I'm walking and thinking, I don't even know why that was the wrong thing to say, but it sure was.

"Goodbye, Mr. Everett." I want to say more than that but it would be a big mistake, I can tell.

"Boone!"

His voice is louder than I've ever heard it. He' still got his back to me.

"Yes, sir?"

"Don't talk about my family again, you hear?"

I nod and then realize he can't see me. "I won't. Sorry."

"Just go on home."

I'm at the door by now and I open it, step through, and close it and the screen.

Chapter Twelve

When I get down off the porch I stop and look back at the house. He told me to do something. What was it? Oh, yeah, I'm supposed to look under the lid of one of the shine jars I've still got when I get home. Okay, I can remember that.

I get home and collapse on the couch. It's not much past the middle of the day and I'm ready for a nap. As I'm dozing off I wonder if Mr. Everett is taking an afternoon nap too. We're like the Mexicans that work out in the fields here, what's that called? Siesta, that's it, siesta. Except I never see these guys take part of the afternoon off, and Daddy was always complaining about how they made him look bad, never stopping, not even for a drink of water, just work, work, work . . . .

I wake up about an hour later with a headache, but at least my head is more or less clear. I sit up and try to remember my visit with old man Everett.

He knew about shine. He knew about the still. He never said so straight out, but I could tell he knew. And he told me to do something. The jar lids, on the shine I've got in the kitchen. I'm supposed to look under the lid.

I go into the kitchen and get one of the full jars and unscrew the lid. When I turn it over it's just shiny metal like all the other lids I've ever seen.

Then, right next to the rubber ring that runs around the outside, I see scratches in the metal. I carry it out the kitchen door, into the afternoon sun, and angle it so I can see what they are. They're blocky, like they were scraped there with a pocketknife, but they're readable.

GAM12 and a star.

The rest of the jars have the same thing scratched into the underside of the lids.

I put all the lids back on tight and put the jars in a cabinet that's got Momma's canning jars in it. Half a dozen jars plus the one I'm working on plus whatever's up there if I can get the old man to show me how it's done. The more I think about this the more excited I get. I go back to the cabinet and pull out all Momma's empty jars and line them up on the counter. There's eighteen of them. That's four and a half gallons, just about enough for everything that's up there at the still. Like I know how much that'll make.

I bet I could sell this stuff.

I know I could sell this stuff. No way I'd sell it to those kids at school; they don't know how to keep their mouths shut about anything. Somebody else.

First, though, I need to learn how to use that still. I'm pretty sure Mr. Everett can help me, but I think I need to give him a day or so to settle down before I go back up.

An hour or so later, the phone rings and I pick it up, trying to sound like I don't feel good in case it's somebody from school. It's the middle of the evening, and I don't think anybody's going to bother me at this time of day, but better safe than sorry.

"Hello?"

"Boone, is that you? You sound awful!"

I can't figure out who it is, but the voice sounds familiar. Since I don't know, I keep up the pretense.

"Yeah, kind of a rough afternoon."

"Is that why you weren't at school today? I was thinking you just decided to skip. Again."

Nancy. I finally figure out who it is and drop the act.

"Maybe not that rough an afternoon. I was looking in on old man Everett and time got away from me."

She laughs. "Yeah, I bet. It's okay, Boone, whatever. I just thought, I mean, I wondered if you were sick, that's all." She pauses for a minute. "You don't have to explain anything to me."

"I'm feeling pretty good now, actually."

"Something happened today." She sounds like she can't wait to tell me something, so I just wait.

"Don't you want to know what it is?"

"I guess, but school stuff is pretty boring, you know?"

Nancy laughs again. She's got kind of a nice laugh.

"Nothing to do with school. I didn't go today. Know why?"

"I don't know. You're sick? I mean for real sick?"

"Nope."

There's a long pause.

"I got my license, and Mom said I could go anywhere in the county as long as I was the only one in the car."

"That's great, Nancy, really." I'm wondering why she's telling me this. She's a smart kid, good grades and all that, and her family isn't rich, but they do okay.

"So, I can go pretty much anywhere in the county now."

I finally get it.

"Maybe I could show you around the farm sometime." Everywhere except that one field and the still. The pool might be nice. I've thought off and on about taking a girl up there, but never had anybody in mind. I always thought they'd have a great body

122

and almost nothing on, and beyond that I hadn't given it much thought. I know that there's guys in school that could talk any of the girls up there, but I'm not one of them.

"Maybe you could."

And now I don't know what to say. I'm deciding that Nancy might be somebody I'd like to show the pool to, but I don't know how to do this kind of thing.

"So what are you doing tomorrow?"

It takes me a second to realize that I said that.

Nancy doesn't hesitate. "I can't give you a ride home from school, but I can tell Mom you need help with your English, which I'm sure you do. How about right after school?"

"Okay."

"Okay, then. See you tomorrow."

She hangs up and I just sit there for a minute. Then I think, I wonder if she drinks shine?

That Wednesday I don't go to school, like usual, but I do check and make sure I have another one of those frozen pizzas in case Nancy is still here when it's time to eat. The place looks okay, so I go check the pool.

The path is a little grown up but easy, at least for me. The creek and pool are just as nice, just as peaceful as I remember, and I'm thinking it's a really good place to take a girl. I decide to sit down for a minute and before I know it it's past time for school to be out, and I dash down the path and into the back yard just in time to see Nancy pulling out onto the road. I wave and shout as loud as I can, and she just keeps driving.

She gets to the top of the hill and stops. I'm still standing in the yard, and I guess she sees me, because she pulls into the Jenkins driveway and turns around. When she gets back in the yard I'm standing there at the kitchen door.

She gets out, in jeans and a tee shirt that says "Eat a Peach" on it and I guess she notices me staring at her chest. She blushes a little and folds her arms over the writing and says, "Dad used to like a band, the Allman Brothers, I never heard of them, but he's too fat to wear his old tee shirts now."

"Oh," I say. I've never heard of them either, and I'm thinking what a stupid thing to put on a shirt, but I don't say it because Nancy looks good in a tee shirt. She's bigger than a lot of girls at school, but not so big they look fake, like Samantha. Sam's a senior and word is all the seniors have had a close-up look at her. I'm trying to stop staring at Nancy and I have to make myself look somewhere else, so I point to the kitchen door and say, "You want something to drink or anything?"

"That'd be nice," she says, and sounds like she's relieved that I can do something besides stare at her boobs.

"Okay, come on in," I say, and remember to let her go in first.

She takes a look around and I can tell she's trying to think of something polite to say. Finally she says, "I should say hello to your mother. Is she in the other room?"

"She's not here," I say, and watch her face change.

"Not here? I thought she didn't have a job, and pretty much stayed home."

"She left, went to her sister's and took Hannah with her. She and Daddy had a fight, he took off, and then she left and they're both gone for good, as far as I know."

"So we're here alone?"

"Yeah, just you and me."

She gets a real funny look on her face and finally says, "Well, I didn't expect that. Maybe I should go."

"Why?" I say.

She gives me a look. "You know why. My Mom would kill me if she knew."

"I'm not going to tell her. Are you?"

Nancy looks at me, right in the eyes, and says, "If you think I'm going to risk getting in that much trouble you're so wrong. I mean, I like you, but I just got this license, Boone. I'm not going to get it taken away already."

I nod. Can't really argue with that, even though I want to. I had the whole thing built up in my head, her following me up to the pool, maybe she'd slip on a rock and I'd put my hand out to catch her, she'd hold on to keep from slipping, and . . . . No use thinking about it, I tell myself. Nothing is going to happen today, no kiss, no getting under that shirt, nothing. I feel myself getting angry, and I go to the door and open it hard.

"Guess you'd better get out of here, then."

"I'm sorry, Boone, really, I want to stay but — "

"Don't want you in any trouble. Just so you know, any time you come up here it'll be just you and me, so I guess I won't see you anymore." I'm holding the door and looking down at the steps, just waiting for her to leave.

"Okay, then, see you at school," she says, a little sad.

"I guess," I say, and watch her go back to her car.

Chapter Thirteen

When she's gone, I go back inside and slam the door hard. I look around for something to throw and catch myself. That's what Daddy used to do, I tell myself, you don't want to be like that, Boone, you know how bad that can get.

I'm still mad, though, so I go out into the barn and get the maul and go out to where Daddy had some rounds cut but not split. I might need wood for the still, and here all this wood is just laying around.

I set the first one up and take a swing, not aiming or anything, just bringing the maul down on the wood as hard as I can. The shock of it hitting damn near pops my arms out of my shoulders, and I look to see that the axe blade of the maul head is pointing up to the sky, and the sledgehammer end is on the wood. It made a little dent, but that's it.

I stare at the wood, not knowing whether to laugh, cry, or throw the maul into the field in front of me. I end up laughing, looking around to make sure nobody saw me, thinking about how long it would be before I would be willing to tell this on myself, and pretty soon I wasn't mad at Nancy anymore.

Tomorrow, I think I'll go see Mr. Everett again, maybe take him a little more shine, and ask him about that GAM12 on the inside of the jar lids.

The next day I'm up early, which for me nowadays is eight thirty, and I eat the last of the dry cereal and have a cup of coffee. Never drank coffee before Momma left, but I'm starting to like it pretty well. I take it black; tried milk in it and didn't like it. I sit out on the steps and watch the road, which is empty almost all the time, like usual, and think about last night.

Last night I dreamed that Frankie was still alive, that that awful day two years ago had never happened, and he was here with me. I dreamed that he had helped me with Daddy after Momma and Hannah had taken off and Daddy had blown his head off out in the barn, and that we were in the shine business and were making tons of money. Nancy kept coming around, and I kept telling her that Momma and Daddy were gone and she should go on home. She'd run off crying and then the dream would change and she and Samantha were here and Frankie and I were slipping shine into their drinks. Then Frankie went into the back room with Samantha and she ran out screaming and I went in

128

and Frankie was torn up something awful, blood and brains and stuff everywhere, and then it was Daddy back there, and everybody was screaming and that's what woke me up.

I shake my head, angry, trying to make that last scene go away. I hate dreams like this, and dreams with Frankie in them especially. The coffee is cold and I take it back inside to get a refill, and this time I add just a touch of shine to it.

With a hot cup of coffee in hand, I go out to the burial site just to have a look. I can barely see it, things are so grown up, and I hesitate for a second before I decide to walk out into the field for a closer look. I can only get half a dozen steps into the field before I see my first kudzu leaf, and the closer I get to where Daddy is buried, the thicker the kudzu gets. The mound is almost settled, and the bare earth is covered. This might work out okay. I take another drink and shake out the last few drops onto the ground.

I can hear the phone ringing when I get back to the yard, but by the time I open the kitchen door it has stopped. I put the cup in the sink and get another little jar from the cabinet and fill it with shine. Mr. Everett should appreciate this.

When I get up to his house I go up and knock on the door. It swings open on its own and I call out, "Mr. Everett, it's Boone from down the hill." There's no answer. I call again — nothing. I look all over; it's a small house, just the living room, the first one I saw him in, all dark and sad-looking, and the hallway to the room in back with all the windows. There's a kitchen and a bedroom, all empty, and a couple of closets. I don't bother with those.

The room with the windows has a door to the outside, so I step out into the back yard. Not much of a yard, really, mostly trees and vines and a path to the toolshed. There are a couple of bird feeders in the trees, probably homemade, and a red wheelbarrow on its side almost covered with vines. The toolshed door is closed, and I go there next.

Nobody home, but it looks like somebody was here not long ago. There's some fresh sawdust on the floor, and some pieces of wood laid out on the bench. I can't tell what they're supposed to be or what the finished product will look like. I go back out into the yard and look around. There's another path, one I didn't see earlier, that leads away from the house and curls around the toolshed before disappearing over a little hill.

I take the path, and just over the little hill I see Mr. Everett. He's heading away from me and it doesn't look like he heard me, so I step back into the shade of a tree and watch until he's almost out of sight. Then I follow, not too close. I didn't know the old guy ever left his house, and I'm curious about where he's going.

He's out of sight over that hill and I speed up to get to the top before he disappears, but I'm too late. When I get to the crest of the hill he's nowhere to be seen. I stand there for a second, looking left, right, then left again, and I'm trying to decide whether to go on back to his house or follow the trail just to see where it leads when I see Mr. Everett coming towards me. He's not on the trail, at least not the same trail I'm on, and he is definitely on Thompson land.

Off in the distance I hear a faint noise that's getting louder, and I recognize it as the four-wheeler that Mrs. Thompson was on when we had our little conversation the other day. Sounds different, somehow, and pretty soon it's clear that there are at least two, maybe three of them. It's also clear that they're headed this way.

Mr. Everett hears it too, and looks toward the noise before quickening his pace, heading cross-country toward a fence that I"m guessing is the boundary between Thompson land and Everett land. Looks like he's going to make it okay and I head back down the trail to his house. I figure he might be thirsty when he gets back.

It takes a lot longer for him to show up than I think it should, and I'm about ready to go looking when there he is, standing at the corner of the house furthest away from the toolshed. Where he comes from I'm not sure; one second there's nobody and the next there he is. I wave and he looks confused and then I guess he recognizes me and raises a hand. All of a sudden I notice how tired he looks and I go over to him to offer him some help. I'm almost to him when he takes a deep breath, straightens up some, and waves me off.

"Don't treat me like a damn cripple, Boone, I'm okay."

I smile at him and he looks like he's about ready to smile back and then it's like he remembers he's supposed to be grumpy or something. "I mean it," he says, but I can tell his heart's not in it. I stay a couple of steps back and we head back to his back door.

When we get inside I pull out the jar and he says, "I was hoping you'd bring some more of that. I finished the other off already. You can take your jar back when you leave."

"All right." I set the little jar on the kitchen counter and look around. It's a small kitchen, smaller than mine, and not much in the way of cabinets. I guess where the glasses might be and get it right the second time. I find two that sort of match and turn to Mr. Everett. "You want some water or something in these?"

He's looking at me like I'm about to strangle his favorite pet. "You don't mix shine with anything, boy. Didn't your daddy teach you anything? Put those glasses back."

He sits down in what is clearly his chair and motions to me. "Bring that jar over here."

I do what I'm told, put the glasses back in the cabinets and carry the jar over and hand it to him. He takes it from me and raises it in a kind of toast and takes a sip. Nodding, he hands it to me and I raise the jar to him and take a sip.

"Have a seat," he says, and I do.

So we sit and talk and sip and it's a fine way to spend an hour or three. I remember from the last time not to mention his family, and he doesn't mention mine. Eventually the talk drifts around to the still I told him about that last visit.

"Say you found the still?"

"Yeah, up in the woods. I don't know how to run one, but there's an old nail keg up there that's about full of something that'll knock you right on your ass if you take a good whiff of it."

He laughs out loud. "Best not stick your nose in that, boy. What are you going to do with that still?"

Here we go, I think to myself. He's as much as asking me if I want to get that thing going again, and I sure would like to.

"I don't know, Mr. Everett, I don't want to get the law after me."

He smiled that same kind of smile I saw the last time, the kind of scary one.

"You know they've got all kinds of stuff to worry about these days, what with meth labs in every other trailer and all that shit kids put into their arms these days. You'd have to be careful, and not sell any, or not sell much, if you didn't want the law snooping around. Not like Popcorn; that old boy had hundreds of gallons set to go the last time they busted him. That little thing on your land won't produce more than a few gallons at a time."

I look him right in the eye. "So you've seen it?"

"Hell, boy, I built it, eight or nine years ago, you were just a little kid."

Somehow I'm not surprised at this. He continues.

"Your daddy was okay with me putting it on his land as long as I gave him a jar every now and then. That worked for a long time, until I started getting a little old and wanted more help from him than just keeping his mouth shut about it being on his property. He started getting ideas about selling it and making it bigger, and all I wanted was just some sipping whisky and I was getting a little old to be swinging a maul and hauling wood and mash up into the woods. I just wanted a little help, you see. We were never up there at the same time, safer that way.

He'd split and carry wood and make sure I had enough of everything to make mash. He'd come up here every now and then, when he knew I had finished a batch, and get his share. Before you told me he had taken off I was starting to wonder a little. He hadn't checked to see if I needed anything, and I could tell he hadn't been up there."

I nod. I could see Daddy being a real asshole about that kind of thing, and, to be fair, he couldn't swing an axe, not with that hand, and he couldn't haul much either. So I can see his side of it, him wanting a bigger share of what was coming out of the still.

Mr. Everett is saying, "We didn't do much this year, not much at all, and that keg you talked about, that's going to have to be thrown out real soon if somebody doesn't do something with it."

I take a sip and hand it across. "Do something with it like what? I don't know how to do anything with it."

"Looking to learn?"

I don't want to come across like some kid, but I want to jump up and say show me show me please. I try to be cool about it and say, "Sure, if you want to teach me, I'm willing."

And he says okay.

Chapter Fourteen

The next week is like going to school with only one subject, something like chemistry, but a lot more fun. He and I sit in his sunny room and talk and sip for the first couple of days, and then we meet at the still. He comes in from one direction, me from another.

He pulls the lid off the nail keg and sniffs, then shakes his head.

"It won't be much good, but it's a shame to pour it out. Besides, might stink up the whole county. The Thompsons would sure be able to smell it. It'll be good for you to practice on, I guess."

He takes me through the whole process, how to build a fire that doesn't put off a lot of smoke, how to read weather signs to know about wind and rain and stuff like that, and how to listen for noises that don't belong in the woods. We have to take off once, in two different directions again, when I think I hear something coming. It turns out to be nothing, but Mr. Everett isn't mad at all. He says better to get it wrong half a dozen times than to stop paying attention and end up getting caught.

The hardest part is throwing away the first little bit that comes out of the coil. I want to taste it right away, but he says that first stuff is poison because the liquid isn't hot enough yet. He's been right about all of it, at least so far, so I take it out away from the still and dump and I don't even have a taste.

Then the first real shine starts coming out and it's so slow I want to do something, anything to speed it up, and he laughs at me and says, "You got the patience of one of those little dogs I saw in town once, going a mile a minute from one thing to another. Bet you watch TV with the clicker in your hand, just going from one thing to another. You need to slow down, boy. Your daddy was impatient, too. This whole thing taking so long drove him crazy. You heard anything from him? He coming back?"

I shake my head, still watching the fire.

"Well, if and when he does come back, I'll let you deal with him. Not going to come between a boy and his daddy. It'll be your fight."

He's not coming back, ever. I think it but don't say it.

Mr. Everett takes a small sip of the finished product and spits it out. "No good," he says. "Needs filtering."

"How long does that take?" I'm ready to be done with this.

"A while," he says. "We'll do it down at my house."

It takes half a dozen trips to get all the shine down to Mr. Everett's house, where he takes a gallon bucket into the toolshed, motioning me to follow him.

At the back of the shed is a glass jar, looks like it would hold a couple of gallons, with a big funnel resting on top and some thick paper and a box of something black.

"Fold the filter paper so it fits into the funnel." Mr. Everett says while he slices the top off the box with a box cutter.

When I do he pours about a quarter of the box into the filter and says, "Charcoal cleans it out, improves the taste. This stuff really needs to have the taste improved."

He points to the gallon of shine. "Pour it into the funnel. Nice and slow."

I do and the funnel fills to about an inch from the top.

"Good," he says. "Now let's go back to the house. This will take a while."

I can tell that by what's coming out of the tip of the funnel. Drip, drip, drip.

I look around and he's grinning at me. "Not like going to the store for a six-pack, is it? Don't worry, the hard part's over now."

He turns and heads back to his house and I follow.

It takes a couple of days to finish the filtering. Mr. Everett filters one of the gallons three times, telling me it's for special occasions. The rest of it's for sipping.

We're sitting in his back room enjoying the fall sun, sipping and talking; it's early fall in the mountains just to our east and there's an occasional nip in the air down here too. I lean back and stretch and say, "You know I wondered the first time I brought the shine up here what you'd do. I was afraid you'd toss me out or call the law on me. This worked out a lot better."

He doesn't say anything for a while. Then he says, "I thought about it, you being young and all, and then I thought about when I was your age. I was already running shine for my daddy. When I remembered that I thought what the hell."

I laugh, and he joins me after a minute.

"What the hell," I say.

"So you used to sell it, I mean your daddy did? And you were the runner?"

He nods. Then he's quiet for a while and finally says, "You going to tell me what really happened to your daddy?"

I stop with the jar halfway to my mouth. Does he know? How could he know? I bring the jar up to my lips and take a sip, then set it back down.

"What do you mean?"

"I mean you know more than you're telling. I can see that, being with you all this time. If you want to keep it to yourself that's fine, I'm just asking the question."

Damn, I think. He knows. But I didn't kill Daddy, he did that to himself. I just buried the body, cleaned up the mess. I didn't really do anything wrong. He would have wanted to be buried on the property.

"I don't know what kind of shape he's in right now and don't much care. He's out of my life. So how's your family? Haven't seen your daughter around for a long time."

"I'll tell you what," he says, and there's anger in his voice I've not heard before. "I won't ask you what happened to your daddy or your little brother, and you don't ask me about my family. Understand?"

I nod. Good, that's good. I don't care about his family and don't want to talk about mine.

We sit in silence for a bit, and then I get up and say, "I need to get back to the house. I might go to the store later. You need anything?"

He stands up too. He's half a head shorter than me, and kind of hunched over. I figure before he started stooping like that he and I would be eye to eye.

"Didn't mean any harm earlier. Didn't mean to snoop into your business, Boone. Okay?"

I give him a smile. "Sure thing, Mr. Everett. Already forgotten. So you need anything from town?"

"One thing," he says. "I'm getting tired of you calling me Mr. Everett. I appreciate the respect, but I'd rather you call me by my given name."

Well. I guess I never thought of him as anything but old man Everett or Mr. Everett. It is true that we're kind of equals in this shine-making, so it feels okay to do that, but I'm not used to calling my elders by their given name.

"I guess that would be all right," I say slowly. "You sure? Feels kind of disrespectful."

"Hell, Boone, I know you respect me. I wouldn't have brought it up if I didn't mean it. I feel old enough already without you going around Mr. Everett this and Mr. Everett that and yes sir and no sir. It'd make me feel better."

"Okay," I say.

"Gamaliel," he says.

What the hell kind of name is Gamaliel? I never heard of such a thing, but I know back years ago people had weird names. I heard about a man, two towns over, first name was Othel. Gamaliel sure sounds better than Othel.

"Gamma - sorry, say it again?"

"Gah - may - lee - ell."

"Gamaliel. Okay. That a family name?"

He shakes his head. "Look it up sometime in your history book."

I go on home, thinking, Gamaliel, what a name.

It hits me after I get home and store the last few jars of the new batch I brought with me. I'm looking at the cabinet almost full and thinking that I've got enough to do through the winter and maybe enough to sell a little and I realize what the scratches on the inside of the lid stand for. I get one of the new ones out just to check and when I unscrew it and turn it over, I don't see the same thing I saw before.

GB13.

Well, I'll be damned, I say to myself. He's gone and made me a partner.

Chapter Fifteen

The next few days I spend just relaxing, getting the last of the vegetables in from Momma's garden. She had harvested most of what there was this year before she took off, but the pepper plants and one tomato plant are still hanging in there, so I bring in what's ripe and decide I'm not going to worry about the rest. There's only so many peppers I can eat.

I check the mail about once a week now and throw out almost all of it as soon as I get in the house. There isn't much comes to us besides junk, and still nothing from Momma. Maybe she said everything in that first letter she wanted to say, but it still feels bad, her leaving me like that.

Gamaliel and I spend time together every other day or so. I still haven't told him about Daddy, but I think he's suspicious. The old guy is pretty sharp.

I'm on the way up to his place and I'm surprised to find a car in the driveway. It takes me a second to recognize it as his daughter's car. When I knock on the door she is the one that opens it.

"Hello. Boone, isn't it?"

"Yes, ma'am. I haven't seen you in a while."

She shakes her head. "No, not for a while. How are you and Pop getting along?"

I nod my head. "Gamaliel is a good guy. I come up a few times a week and we spend a little time together."

Her eyebrows arch. "Gamaliel? How did you find out about that?"

I shrug. "Guess it was my fourth or fifth visit. He told me to stop calling him Mr. Everett, told me to call him Gamaliel. When I asked him about it, cause it's kind of a strange name, he said look it up."

"And did you?"

"No, not yet." I am a little embarrassed. "I keep meaning to, but just never got around to it."

"It's got a lot of history to it, like Boone."

She is surprised when I start laughing. "My name doesn't come from the guy in the books," I say after a moment. "Momma told me it was because she and Daddy really liked Boone's Farm Apple wine when they were younger, I guess when they were, well, when they were . . . ." I let the words trail off; I don't want to talk to this woman about my parents making me after splitting a bottle of Boone's Farm. Just thinking about my parents doing it at all makes me a

144

little sick to my stomach. Old people and sex. Not that I know anything about it. Nancy never came back around, and I think about calling her and don't do it, so who knows when I will know something?

Gamaliel's daughter is hiding a smile behind one hand, then straightens up and says, "I'm glad you came by, Boone, we need a favor."

Oh boy, here we go. Wonder what it is she wants. I'm not much on doing favors for people; usually it turns out to be a lot bigger than they say it's going to be, and I don't like making promises anyway.

"Okay," I say slowly. "What kind of favor?"

"Pop needs some tests run at the hospital over in Nashville, and we were hoping you could look in on the house while he's staying with us."

"What kind of tests?" Gamaliel seems healthy enough to me. I don't like doctors, haven't been to one in a long time, and hospitals, well, Frankie died in a hospital. I really don't like hospitals.

"Just some blood work, and his daddy had eye problems and we want to make sure he gets looked at every year or so. Pop doesn't like hospitals much."

"When are you leaving?"

"That's why I said I was glad you came by. Saves us the trouble of stopping by your house. He's packing some clothes right now."

I hear Gamaliel's voice from inside. "Boone, is that you?"

"Yeah, Gamaliel, it's me."

"Come on in here, boy. I need to talk to you."

I look at her and she shrugs. "Maybe he wants to tell you about taking care of the place. Go on in, he's back in the bedroom."

She steps back and I go in, down the hallway, and turn right into the bedroom. I haven't really been in here before, I always just walk on by on my way to the kitchen or the sunroom. I stop at the doorway and look in.

Gamaliel is sitting on the side of his bed, a small one, looks barely big enough for him to sleep on. There's a suitcase on the bed, open, with some clothes in it and a jar. I smile at the jar.

He sees what I'm looking at and motions me on in. When I get close enough he whispers, "Don't tell her, you hear?"

I shake my head, still smiling. He stands up and says, real quiet, "There's a couple of things you need to know, Boone.

"I know she told you that this was just for some tests, but she and that husband of hers have been trying to get me out of this house for years. They have a room at their place and every time they get me off the property they start in on me about moving in with them. It'll be the same this time, I know it will."

"Hell, Gamaliel, you're doing just fine here. Tell her no."

"I do, every time. It gets harder and harder for her to hear it, seems like. Anyway, you know all that work we did together?"

I nod. There's stuff in the house and in the shed.

"You move that stuff, at least part of it, down to your barn. I've raised such hell every time before that they've given up and brought me back, but she's getting stubborn about it."

Wonder where she learned that, I say to myself. Gamaliel and I haven't had any fights about anything we've been doing, but I bet he'd be like an old dog with a piece of meat in its jaws if he set his mind on something.

I nod but don't say anything, because I can hear footsteps in the hall. In a second she's in the doorway.

"Ready to go, Pop? It's kind of a drive, and your first appointment is in a few hours."

"I'll be there in a minute," he says irritably. "Go on and get the car turned around. Boone'll help me with this suitcase."

She shakes her head and goes on out. In a second we hear the screen door close.

He hands me a key. "Don't spill any," he says with a grin. "Remember all that work."

"I won't," I take the key and put it in my pocket. "Won't be long before we'll be working on next year's batch."

Gamaliel nods. "I'd like that, Boone. Truly I would."

He's got a look on his face I can't quite identify. Then it passes and he says, "Get that case and let's go before she comes back in here and starts poking at me."

I laugh. "You'd never let her get away with that, Gamaliel."

He shakes his head. "You just wait til you're old."

We go down the hallway and out the door. I put the suitcase in the trunk and Gamaliel gets in the passenger's seat. She's already in the driver's seat and when I close the trunk she starts the engine.

"Thanks, Boone," she says and waves out the window. I wave back and watch them pull out onto the road and disappear over that first hill.

I lock the door and head back to the house. Going out to the barn, I take a look around. The truck takes up quite a bit of room, but there's a little room off to the side with slatted walls, just about four feet wide and six feet long. A long time ago it was a corn crib, at least that's what Daddy told me. The walls were made of old tobacco sticks running longways, about six inches apart. That made it easy for air to circulate through the corn, keep it from molding until it dried out. We never grew corn, but the barn was here when we moved onto the place, and we used the barn for tobacco and the corn crib for storage.

I open the door and step inside. It smells musty, and me stepping in stirs up a lot of dust from the part of the floor that wasn't covered in hay and old blankets. There are some tools in one corner, a post hole digger, a machete leaned against the wall, and the pick and shovel I used to dig the grave. Seeing them stops me for a second, but then I look around a little more.

There's one corner that has old feed sacks and hay just kind of thrown into it, and I'm thinking that would be as good a place as any to stack some of the jars. I go out and look around the rest of the barn and don't see any place that would work better. I return to the corn crib and pull the sacks away from the wall. A couple of mice run away into cracks in the floor.

I go back to the house and I'm getting ready make a sandwich when the phone rings. It makes me jump because it almost never rings.

When I get to it it's still ringing, and I see that it's Nancy's number. I pick up the phone.

"Hello?"

"Boone, where the hell have you been?"

Chapter Sixteen

I have never heard Nancy even excited, much less this worked up.

"Up to a friend's house. I just got back."

"So you don't know what happened at school today."

I hadn't been to school in a while, and nobody had called or come by. I was planning to leave well enough alone.

"No idea."

"Deputy Fife came and hauled Mr. Timmons away in his squad car. Handcuffs and everything. Nobody knows what it's about, but everybody's talking about it."

Mr. Timmons is the shop teacher. He has a reputation of having a gang of seniors that think they run the school and they call him Boss. I think he's got something on the principal; Mrs. Howard won't cross him, and nobody else will stand up to him either. I got on the bad side of one of those seniors my freshman year and barely made it through shop in one piece. I remember Mr. Timmons laughing while his gang chased me around the shop with hammers and two by fours. He was, and is, a real asshole.

"I hope whatever it is, it's something serious. I'd like to see that prick in jail."

"Boone!" Nancy is sometimes kind of sensitive to language, but she doesn't hang up.

"So nobody knows what he's done?"

"Well, there are rumors."

I waited.

"Boone? Are you still there?"

"Yeah, I'm here. I thought you were still talking, something about rumors."

"Oh, okay. Well, some people are saying that he . . . ." She kind of trails off.

"What?" I'm beginning to think that she doesn't know anything. So why did she call? I start to say something when she starts up again.

"They say, well, . . . you know that big lake house he has?"

Everybody knows about Timmons' lake house. It's pretty famous among high school guys, so I think I know what she's about to say.

"Yeah, I've heard of it." I decide to let her tell it; she might know stuff I don't.

"Well, they say he let some of the seniors have parties up there, and sometimes he was there too, and, well, stuff happened that wasn't supposed to."

I don't say anything. Nancy is really uncomfortable talking about this, and I kind of enjoy that. So I let her talk, see how much she'll say.

"You know what I mean, Boone?"

"Maybe, I'm not sure. What kind of stuff?"

There's a long silence. Then, "They say that they took girls up there, and there was drinking, and, you know."

"What kind of drinking?"

"They say all kinds, beer and wine and moonshine and everything."

"Really? They say anything else?" I'm starting to wish Nancy was here in the house with me telling me all this.

"I heard that some girls, you know, went swimming with the guys and, you know, didn't get dressed right after they came out of the lake."

I'm definitely wishing Nancy was up here.

"And?"

"Boone, I can't talk about this on the phone. I'm red as a beet right now."

"You ever drink beer, Nancy?"

She doesn't say anything for a minute. Then she says, "Once, at my cousin's house, last summer."

"So what'd you think?"

"I just had one sip, I don't think I liked it much."

"What about moonshine?"

"I wouldn't even know where to go to taste any of that stuff."

I do. I almost say it out loud, and then wonder why I didn't.

"What about you? Would you even know where to go to taste some, Boone?"

I can't believe she's asking me that.

"Well, here." I say, and then hold my breath. Did I just make a huge mistake?

"Boone! Are you serious?"

I nod, and then realize she can't see me. "Yeah, I found some Daddy had hidden in the barn, and he's been gone so long I don't think he's coming back."

She says real fast, "I gotta go," and hangs up. I hang up slow, shaking my head at the phone.

You've really done it now, Boone, I say to myself. What the hell were you thinking?

The phone rings.

"So did you taste it?"

I'm smiling into the phone. Maybe not a huge mistake. I've been dying to tell somebody about this, and any of the guys, well, they'd come up here and it'd be gone in one night and they'd probably burn down the house and the barn while they were at it. Nancy may be willing to keep quiet about it.

"Yeah, I did."

"What was it like?"

I really don't know what to do here. For one crazy minute I wish Gamaliel were here to give me advice, then I think, no, he's like a hundred years old, he probably can't remember. Then I know that's not true, I'll bet his memory is just fine. Anyway, he's not here. You're on your own, Boone.

"It's really strong. I like to mix it up with some Thunderstorm Soda — you know, an S&S — shine and soda." I just made that up, but I like the sound of it.

"Would you let me try it?"

This is not happening to me, I think to myself.

"You have to promise not to tell anybody. Not even your girlfriends. Okay?"

"I promise."

"I mean it, Nancy. I don't want any trouble, I'm taking a chance telling you. I need to be able to trust you on this."

"You can't see me, but I'm crossing my heart."

"That's good. So describe it to me. What are you wearing?"

"Boone, you should be ashamed of yourself!" She hangs up, but it sounded like she was laughing when she did.

I decide that a drink would be really good right now.

Over the last few weeks I've gotten into the habit of watching movies and cop shows on TV, but today I make it a point to turn on the local news. Usually I could give a damn about that kind of thing, but after Nancy's phone call, I'm thinking Mr. Timmons might be on TV.

And there he is, walking down the school steps, Deputy Fife beside him, and a big crowd of students right behind him. He doesn't look good; I think he knows his gang of seniors might not be able to help him. Hell, they might help bring him down.

The followup story says that half a dozen juveniles have also been taken into custody. Briefly I wonder about Curt, but then think, well, too bad for him. He wanted to run with the big boys.

I turn off the TV and go into the kitchen. Much as I hate to, I have to think about money. I get out the money from all the places I've stashed it around the house and dump it on the table, then sit down and count it.

From six hundred I'm down to two hundred and fifteen. There is no way I can make it through the winter with two hundred dollars. Then I remember the eighty dollars Gamaliel's daughter gave me. I had it when I went up to Gamaliel's house and laid it out on his table. I remember he picked it up and threw it on the floor, but I never picked it up. I couldn't see him just throwing money away or doing something stupid like burning it. I wonder if it's in his house somewhere. I could really use that money, and I've bought stuff for Gamaliel, so it's not like I'd be stealing from him. I used my money when I should have been using that.

The next day I'm standing in his kitchen looking around. I'm up here to move some of the shine back to my barn; Gamaliel hasn't come back yet, which worries me a little, and I've still got a few gallons to move, including the triple filtered stuff that Gamaliel hasn't let me sample. "You won't believe it," he tells me over and over, like he's tried it. "Needs to be a special occasion."

I'll get the last of it moved today and tomorrow. Right now I need to find that money. I stand in the middle of the kitchen and turn around slow, thinking where would he put that? I think he'd just stuff it somewhere and not be all that careful with it. Maybe a drawer?

I start opening drawers in the kitchen. Utensils, more utensils, three junk drawers, one with an old phone book and some loose paper in it. No money, no envelope that might have money in it.

The sunroom is right next to the kitchen, so I go in there. Not much in here, just a few of those homemade chairs and a couple of end tables.

The end table next to the chair he always sits in has three or four books on top. One of them is a Bible.

Funny, I never thought of Gamaliel as a religious man. I pick it up and thumb through it. Never read it all the way through, even though Momma kept after me to. "There's good advice in there, son," she'd say to me and I'd just nod and go back to whatever I was doing.

There's no advice in this Bible about where there might be some money. Same for the other books. I open the drawer in the end table.

There's a pistol in there, which surprises me until I think about him living up here on his own.

And there's a box.

Chapter Seventeen

A plain wooden box, nice woodworking, some kind of clear finish on what I'm thinking is walnut. I'll bet Gamaliel made this out in his shop. There's no lock, no hasp of any kind. The box doesn't seem all that heavy when I pick it up and carry it into the kitchen. I set it down on the kitchen table and pull out a chair.

When I open the lid, I just stare into it for a long time.

The eighty dollars is there, the bills smoothed out and stacked neatly on top of all the other money. I take a deep breath. Looks like Gamaliel doesn't trust banks.

After hesitating for a moment, I take the four twenties out and put them in my pocket. Then I just stare at the rest. Rolls of bills, held together with rubber bands, I count eight of them. I wonder how much is in each roll.

Only one way to find out, I think to myself. I pick up one of the rolls and pull the rubber band off. The money stays curled but opens out just a little. It must have been in that roll for a long time. I'm a little reluctant to touch it again, but curiosity gets the better of me and I pick it up.

It's all tens, as far as I can tell at first glance, and I start counting. There are forty-eight of them.

My hands shake a little when I realize that there are seven more rolls. That comes to, and it takes me a second because fifty would have been a lot easier, over thirty-eight hundred dollars, $3,840.00 to be exact. I roll up the bills and break the rubber band trying to put it back on. There are half a dozen rubber bands in the box and I grab one and wrap it around the bills. When I put the roll back in I notice something and this time I have to sit down. The rolls aren't all the same.

There's two rolls of ones, at least the outer bill is a one, two rolls of fives, then the tens I just counted, then one each of twenties, fifties, and hundreds. I can't even do the math without a pencil and paper and maybe a calculator, but I'm guessing there's fifteen thousand dollars there at least. I'm tempted to unroll each one and see if all the bills are alike, to see what I've got here, when I realize what just happened.

In my head I said what I've got here. This isn't your money, Boone, I say sternly to myself, and that doesn't work at all, so I try it out loud.

"This isn't your money, Boone," I say as firmly as I can.

Then I put the lid back on the box and put it back in the drawer before that doesn't work either. I take the eighty dollars and the last two gallons of shine and head back to the house.

When I pull the truck into the barn I just sit there for a minute, breathing hard, thinking about all that money. What if Gamaliel doesn't come back? Does his daughter know about all that money? Maybe I should get it out of there and hide it down here somewhere, keep it safe. I've never had a problem like this before, ever in my life. Daddy always was screaming about money, Momma was trying to make do on almost nothing, the lights never were off but it was close more than once. There's enough up there for me to last years, the way I'm used to spending money.

"But it's not mine, and Gamaliel, he's okay, always treats me right, he needs that money or he wouldn't have it stashed right there in his house." I'm talking to myself and I don't care, I got nobody else to talk to, not about this.

Not about anything, really.

And that really makes me mad at Momma for leaving and taking Hannah and I'm mad at Frankie for dying and I'm really mad at Daddy for being such a nasty old drunk and all of a sudden I'm crying, crying, just sitting there in that old truck looking at the last place I saw Daddy.

I'm really scared. What if Gamaliel really doesn't come back? What if the old man dies on me? What'll I do then?

I need to get him to show me how to make mash, how to do that first step, so I can make some more shine when I run out and maybe start selling a little here and there. So he needs to come back. That old man better not die on me. Not yet.

I don't remember going back to the house. I think I had another sandwich for supper, but I'm not sure about that either. I wake up on the couch and sit up and look around and wonder what time it is. The TV remote is next to me and I turn it on. The news comes on and I look outside and figure it's morning. So about seven or so.

It's been a few days since I checked the mail, so I eat a handful of cereal and go out to the mailbox. Junk, junk, junk, and a letter from Momma.

The rest of the mail goes in the trash and I sit down and open the envelope. Inside there's fifty dollars and a short letter.

Dear Son,
     Sorry it's been so long. I wanted to wait til I

could send you a little money.

I hope your daddy's not hurting you too bad. Hannah's doing good in school, and Claire says she's just the prettiest little thing. Hannah says to say hi.

I think Hannah's going to stay with Claire now. You should get up here sometime and see her.

I've met this really nice man, he treats me so good, but he don't want kids around, he wants it to be just him and me, and Claire said I should try to be happy. Jake and I are moving up to Illinois, probably pretty soon now.

They say Chicago's nice, except it gets cold sometimes, and I wish I could take you with me but Jake said it wouldn't work out and, well, I'm going to move to Illinois soon.

You stay in school now and take care of yourself. I love you.

Momma

For a long time I just sit there staring at the letter. Then I go into the living room and wreck it.

The next day I take all the broken furniture out of the living room, all the shattered picture frames and all the little knickknacks that Momma had put all over the place that are all broken now, and I take them to the ditch that runs through the back end of the property and I throw it all in there and then I go back in the house, into the living room, there's just the couch and the TV in there now, and I sit down on the couch and turn on the TV and there's nothing on and I turn it back off and go outside and sit on the back step.

I'm still sitting there an hour later when I hear the phone ring.

It takes me a second to decide that I want to answer it. By the time I reach the phone, I'm thinking it's too late, but I pick it up anyway.

"Hello?"

"Are you going to be nice?"

"Hi, Nancy. I'm sorry for being so curious."

She laughs, and I relax a little.

"I guess curiosity isn't such a bad thing," she says, and I swear I think she's teasing me.

"Did you see the news?" she continues.

"Yeah, Timmons didn't look so good."

"Everybody's saying he's in a lot of trouble, and some of the students too. I guess he had some favorites in the senior class."

"Yeah, I've heard that same thing. Fact is, they came after me once, and Timmons thought it was great fun. Laughed his ass off."

She didn't correct my language this time. "Came after you?"

163

"Just chased me around a little. Nothing, really, but I was a freshman and back then I thought it was a big deal."

"You should tell somebody, Boone."

"No, no, no," I didn't want that spread around the school. I think they've pretty much forgotten about me right now, and I don't want that to change. "You don't tell anybody about that, okay, Nancy? It's not like I was the only freshman they did that to, and, besides, this lake house thing is way bigger than that."

"Well, okay, if you say so. So how are you? You didn't sound too good when you picked up the phone. I was about ready to hang up, and when you did answer, you sounded so sad."

"I'm all right, just missing Momma a little." Now why did I say that? She'll think I'm some kind of baby.

"Where's your mother, Boone? Is she sick?"

"No, she and Daddy got into it a while back and she took off. I don't think she's coming back."

"Oh, Boone, that's awful, I'm so sorry. Who's taking care of you?"

"I guess I am."

Nancy sounded like she was about to cry. "You want me to come over? Have you had supper? We've got plenty, you can come over here."

I have to admit, it feels good to have somebody worry about me. It's been a while. "No, I just had some leftovers, I'm good. Thanks."

"Well, I'm going to put together some snack food and bring it over tomorrow." She had that don't argue with me tone in her voice. "I'll be there pretty soon after school."

"Nancy, I don't want you worrying over me. Don't tell your parents, either, I'm fine, really I am."

"Why don't you want any help, Boone? Pride goes before a fall, you know."

I don't want help because I've got a few gallons of shine stored around here and I don't want anybody snooping around. I don't say that to her.

Instead, I say, "I'm doing okay, really. After all, I'm close to seventeen, be an adult pretty soon. Might as well get used to it."

"Well, I think you need somebody to look after you. Mom and Dad — "

I cut her off. "I don't want any charity from your folks or anybody else. Don't tell, them, Nancy, I'm asking you, don't talk to them about me. Okay?"

She said, "Okay, Boone, If you're sure."

I breathe a sigh of relief. "Yeah, I'm sure. Thanks."

I try to get the conversation onto another subject, because I'm enjoying having somebody to talk to.

165

"You know you're still welcome to come over. I'd like to see you."

"So you'll know what I'm wearing without having to ask?"

And just like that she's all playful again. I'm having trouble keeping up, but I decide to go with it.

"That's it exactly." I realize I'm grinning into the phone.

"You're a mess, Boone, you know that?"

I laugh out loud; can't remember the last time I did that, especially around a girl.

She says, "I gotta go. Some of us have homework. See you, Boone."

"See ya."

I hang up and go back out on the back steps and sit back down, feeling a lot better.

Chapter Eighteen

The next day I see a car go by my place that I don't recognize for a second, then remember it belongs to Gamaliel's daughter. It goes halfway up the hill toward his house and then slowly backs down the hill and turns into my yard. I get a bad feeling in the pit of my stomach.

His daughter and her husband get out and come toward the house. I'm out in the yard already, so I walk up to them. They both stop and wait for me to close the distance between us. As I approach, they exchange looks and she steps forward.

"Hello, Boone."

"Ma'am."

"I guess you've been wondering where Pop has been."

"Yes, ma'am, I have. Is everything okay?"

She hesitates, and I think, the old man's gone. Do they know about the money?

Drawing a deep breath, she says, "Pop's not doing too well."

I relax a little. He's not gone, not yet.

"Is he still in the hospital?"

She nods. "They're going to release him tomorrow. We want you to make sure the house is in good shape for him to come home. I'll be staying with him for a while, but neither of us has the time to make sure there's some food in the refrigerator, that kind of thing. Can you take care of that for us?"

I nod.

"Pop said you should do what's on this list," she hands me a small piece of paper. "I'll stop by tomorrow so you can say hi before we go on up to the house. Pop says thank you and he hopes you can make sure that place where he likes to sit is all cleared out." She frowns a little. "Not sure what he meant by that, but that's what he said."

"I'll take care of it," I say firmly.

I'm pretty sure I know what he meant by that.

She turns to her husband and puts out her hand. He scowls at me, but reaches in his pocket and pulls out some money. She counts off five twenties and hands them to me.

"For the stuff you pick up at the store, and for helping out."

"I'll bring you the change, ma'am," I say, my eyes on her husband. "I won't take money for helping out a

168

friend, but I'll pick up some stuff and have it up at the house tomorrow. What time do you think you'll be here?"

She gives her husband and I-told-you-so look and says, "Not until late afternoon. Thanks, Boone,"

I nod. "Y'all be safe on the roads."

She smiles back; her husband doesn't. They get in the car and head down the road.

I really don't like that guy. Not that I've ever done anything to him.

Back in the house, I pour a drink and sit down with Gamaliel's note.

Boone,

Feeling better. Headed home. Get everything cleaned up, especially around my chair, before I get back. See you soon,

G.

Okay. His chair can only mean one chair, but I'll check in the front room just to be sure. I'm thinking he wants that pistol and box hidden somewhere before he gets there with his daughter and her husband. I'll bet it's the husband he doesn't trust. I sure as hell don't trust him.

I make a quick trip to the store. I've been out on the road enough in the old pickup that nobody even notices me anymore. I get a boxful, milk and bread and sandwich meat and, even though I've never seen him eat any, a couple of cans of soup. His daughter didn't say what was wrong with him; might be a stomach thing. I've got a ziplock bag of chicken soup that Momma made and froze a month or two before she left. I'll take him that.

After unpacking the food, I decide to start in the front room. It's always dark in here, so I open the curtains and turn on all the lights. It doesn't help much.

Gamaliel almost never used this room, but when he did, he sat in the big stuffed chair next to the fireplace. There's an end table next to it, and it's got two drawers in it, so I open the top one.

Nothing but an old word search puzzle book. I don't think he's talking about that kind of thing, so I leave it where it is, close the drawer, and open the second one. It sticks, like it hasn't been opened in a long time.

There's a small metal box, looks like a cash box, in the drawer, and nothing else. I lift the box out of the drawer; it's heavy, and I carry it into the kitchen, set it on the counter, and push back the clasp. When I lift the lid, I understand why it's heavy.

It's half full of silver dollars, more than I've ever seen before. I pick one up and carry it over to where the sunlight is streaming into the room. The date says 1885. I don't know anything about coin collecting, but I'm betting this is worth more than a dollar.

Altogether there are thirty-one silver dollars in the box. I don't look at all the dates, they wouldn't mean much to me anyway, but I figure they're worth something.

I take the box, the pistol, and the box of paper money and put them all into my knapsack, then take that out to the shed and put it under the workbench, back out of sight. Then I lock up the house and head back home.

I'm only there for about an hour before I start thinking. Maybe Gamaliel meant for me to hide the stuff down here at my place. The more I think about it the more sense that makes, so I get back in the truck and make the return drive.

When I get there I'm really glad I came back. There's a four-wheeler parked in the backyard and a couple of guys at the back door, rattling the knob. One of them has a wrench and looks like he's getting ready to break a window. As soon as I see them I start racing the engine and blowing the horn. They don't stop to see who's pulling into the driveway, just jump on the four-wheeler and take off across the field.

Immediately I start toward the shed and then stop; I need to make sure they, whoever they are, are actually gone and not watching me from somewhere close by. I don't want Gamaliel to come home to a house torn apart by a couple of damn thieves, and I don't want to call Deputy Anderson because I think he's pretty much forgotten about me and I want to keep it that way. I've always called him Deputy Fife, like everybody I know, but I'm starting to think I should call him by his real name. The guy's treated me okay over the last few months, not being nosy and accepting what I tell him, and all of a sudden I feel bad for making fun of him like I do. Like everybody does.

This thing with the four-wheeler has me worried a little bit. If there's thieves around, I can't watch both houses at the same time, and I won't feel right leaving Gamaliel alone in his house. Then I remember that his daughter is going to stay with him for a while, and maybe that husband of hers, and that makes me feel a little better. I get out of the truck and go around back, out toward the field they took off across, and look around the best I can. No sign of anybody, no noise besides what noises ought to be there. Good enough. I turn to head back to the house when I catch a light out of the corner of my eye, like a reflection. It's off to the left, kind of back in the trees, and when I look close I can barely make out the four-wheeler. So they're not gone after all.

I step out into the field and point straight at them to let them know I see them, hoping that will make them go away and not come after me. Nothing happens, and I take another step closer.

One guy takes off on foot along the edge of the woods and the other guy fires up the four-wheeler and heads at a right angle to the first, up over the hill, right through the middle of the field. Guess they figure if they split up there's no way I can chase both of them at the same time. They're right, of course.

What they don't know is that I have no intention of chasing either one of them. What I did just then is the biggest bluff I've ever run in my life. I can't believe it worked.

I go back, out of the field, and head for the shed. Reaching under the bench, I grab the backpack and carry it to the truck, toss it in, and take it back down to the house.

The next morning I check to make sure Gamaliel's shine is still in the barn and my knapsack is still in the closet behind the shotgun. I don't like this being responsible for other people's stuff, especially money. I need to see Gamaliel and get him by himself so we can talk about all this.

In the afternoon I go up to his place, open it up, and let some fresh air in. I look around; it's clean, cleaner than my place, so I leave well enough alone and sit down to wait.

And get right back up and go out, almost forgetting to lock the doors, and get back in the truck and head back down to my place. All the stuff I'm supposed to be keeping an eye on is down here, and I can see them coming; they can't get to his place without passing mine.

Seems like it takes forever before I see the car, a late model Chevy, I've seen it enough times to recognize it now, and I start to follow them up the road when a thought hits me.

More a question, really, than a thought. Do I take the backpack with me? Leave it here? Take the pistol and leave everything else? The thought of having the pistol with me is scary and kind of exciting at the same time. I don't want the guys on the four-wheeler to come around while I'm up at Gamaliel's and carry off all the stuff I'm supposed to be watching. I need to think about this, but I need to get up there and tell them about the guys trying to break in, too.

I finally go back in the house, take the backpack out from behind the shotgun, and take it into the living room. I set it down on the floor next to the couch and stare at it, trying to figure out what the hell to do.

Finally I take it with me, pistol in my pocket, and the backpack with the rest of the stuff in it behind the seat of the pickup truck. The shine I leave behind; worse comes to worst, we can make more.

When I get there they're already inside and I go up to the front door and knock. Gamaliel's daughter answers the door, but before she can say anything I hear his voice from the back of the house.

"Carrie! Who is it? Who's at the door?"

She smiles at me and motions me in, turns around and yells, "It's Boone, Pop."

"Tell him to get his ass in here!"

She rolls her eyes and points down the hall. "I imagine you know your way?"

"Yes, ma'am."

She stops me, one hand on my arm. "If you're going to call him Gamaliel, you might as well call me Carrie. Carrie Phillips." She holds out her hand and I take it. She's got a good handshake.

The husband comes down the hall, scowling.

"This is Jerry, my husband."

"Mr. Phillips," he says, and doesn't take my offered hand. I leave it there for a few seconds and then let it drop to my side.

I decide not to make a big deal out of it. "So how is he, Carrie?"

The look on Jerry's face is priceless. "Her name is Mrs. Phillips," he says, sounding really angry.

"Now, Jerry, I told him to call me Carrie," she says, trying to smooth things out.

"I don't want any trouble, Mrs. Phillips," I say, and walk off to say hi to Gamaliel. I can hear them talking behind me, too low for me to hear.

He's sitting in the sunroom in his regular chair. When I come into the room he looks up at me and says, "Where is it?"

I take the pistol out of my pocket and hand it to him. He checks to make sure it's loaded and then points it at my chest. "Where's the rest of it?"

"In the truck. Behind the seat. Everything except the shine. It's all down at the house."

He lowers the pistol and grins at me. "Good boy, Boone."

I grin back. "Good to see you, Gamaliel. Thought you'd run off with a nurse or something."

It's the wrong thing to say. I can tell immediately.

"Sorry, man, I didn't mean anything by it."

He has such a sad look in his eye I almost want to pat his hand and tell him everything is going to be all right. Except he still has that gun in his hand.

Slowly he loses the sad look and then shakes his head. "I know, Boone, I know."

"What are you doing with a gun in this house?" Carrie is standing in the doorway, Jerry right behind her.

Gamaliel waves it in the general direction of the back yard. "It's for protection."

I decide that this is a good time to tell them about what happened yesterday. I start to and then, just as quick, change my mind. I think I'll just keep quiet about it. I don't want to have to talk to the law, I didn't really see anything, everybody's leaving me alone right now and that's how I like it. Maybe I'll tell Gamaliel later on.

I stick around for a few more uncomfortable minutes. Jerry makes no secret of the fact he doesn't like me much, and Carrie can't seem to get him to behave himself, so I just tell the old man I'm glad to see him back and I'll talk to him later.

"Take care of that old truck," he says and gives me a wink.

"I will." I don't return the wink, but there's a smile on my face as I'm leaving.

Chapter Nineteen

I'm not sure I like the way things seem to be heading right now. Gamaliel's all right, but his daughter, and especially her husband, might decide to stick their nose into my business. Nancy, well, I think I might like to get Nancy over here, talk to her, maybe give her a taste of shine, help her understand that I don't need her parents getting all protective of me; I don't want them to make me some kind of charity case. I don't worry so much about anybody finding the grave anymore; doesn't take long around here for vines and brush to take over, and we hadn't used that little field for anything the last year or so anyway. Still, I'm feeling like any day now somebody's going to knock on the door and get real nosy, and I'm not going to know what to do about that. Aside from not having anybody to talk to most of the time, things are good enough that I don't want them to change. Maybe I'll get a dog, a big one. Always wanted a dog.

One other thing that bothers me when I think about it is this house I'm living in, which we never owned. Daddy was more a sharecropper than anything else. Not exactly, since he didn't work this piece of land, except for trying to raise a little tobacco, and Wilcox always took a piece of that. Mr. Wilcox owns a few of these old farmhouses and he told Daddy we could stay here and he'd take the rent out of Daddy's pay. Something about not wanting a bunch of Mexicans in here, how they'd tear the place up and pack all their kin in the house and the barn. He's sure not going to like what Daddy did to the place just before he blew his brains out. I don't think I'll see him; he never came around during the summer or fall. Season's over, so he probably won't throw me out yet, but come spring, he'll give this place to somebody that'll work the fields. I'm not a field hand.

I'll worry about that in the spring, I guess.

The more I think about getting a dog the better the idea sounds. There was that kid at school, every once in a while he'd talk about his bitch having puppies and how he couldn't sell them because he wasn't sure who the daddy was and they couldn't be registered. His dog was a Rottweiler, big for a female, I'd only seen her once but I sure wouldn't mess with her. Wonder if he's got any pups now. What the hell was his name?

Maybe Nancy would know. She always hung around with the good kids and this guy was pretty rough, but she might know his name. I decide to ask her the next time she calls.

She doesn't call for two days. I spend my time hanging out at the house, visiting Gamaliel and trying to stay out of Jerry's way. Carrie and I are starting to get along pretty well, but I don't know about her husband. She and I are sitting in the sunroom with Gamaliel in the afternoon sun when she says, "Boone, do you know how Gamaliel got his name?"

"No, Carrie, I don't," I say, glancing over at the old man. He looks asleep, but I haven't been fooled by that pose in a while. "When he told me his given name and I asked where it came from, he said to look in my history book. I'm not much for history, but I did look in our textbook and there's no Gamaliel in American history. I figure it's European or world history and I'm not sure I'm curious enough to do all that reading." That gets a laugh from the old man, but he doesn't open his eyes.

Carrie smiles. "It actually is American history. The problem with your history book is that they don't give you all the information. You know your presidents?"

I nod. "You mean can I recite them in order? Maybe whenever it was they had us memorize them, what was that, eighth grade? Couldn't do it now to save me."

"Pop was born in 1922. Does that help?"

I do a quick calculation. "He's pushing ninety. That's really old."

He opens his eyes at that one. "You watch yourself, Boone, I'll get up and give you a thrashing."

We all have a good laugh at that, and I say, "Sorry, Carrie, I can't remember who was president then, if that's where you're going with this."

She nodded. "That's where I'm going, exactly. Warren G. Harding was president in 1922. Pop's mother and father were Republicans and they really liked Harding, so when they had a son they named him for the person in the White House."

Gamaliel breaks in. "Nowadays people name their kids after rock stars or football players. Bet you're not named after the explorer, are you Boone? Bet you're named after some athlete or TV star or something like that."

"Now, Pop," Carrie tries to shush the old man. I know that isn't going to work, unless she's a lot better than I am.

"No, not for the explorer," I say, thinking about where Momma told me I got my name.

"So does Gamaliel know where your name comes from?" Carrie wants to know.

When I tell them what Momma told me, there's a long silence, and then Gamaliel starts laughing. I look over at him and he's holding his stomach and almost doubled over. He can't seem to catch his breath, but finally starts to calm down and breathe more normally. He straightens up and wipes his eyes. Looking over at me, he shakes his head and then starts up again and he goes through the same process, a little quicker this time. I'm almost laughing at the old guy myself; never seen him laugh like that. When he straightens up for the second time he looks at Carrie, who is biting her lip, I guess to keep from laughing out loud. I start to thank her for not laughing at me when I hear a voice from the hallway.

"Guess I can start calling you Boone's Farm Boy now."

Jerry is standing there grinning like a fool, pointing at me and nodding his head. I can feel myself getting madder and madder and know I only have a few seconds to get out of there, so I stand up and say, "I'll look in on you real soon, Gamaliel." I start for the door and Jerry says, "Bye, bye, Boone's Farm Boy!"

I catch him right in the throat with my elbow as I'm passing him. He draws in a rasping breath and clutches his throat with both hands. I keep going, but behind me I hear Gamaliel say, "Serves you right,

182

you pompous asshole." Jerry is still making those sucking noises and I turn around just as I'm about to open the front door.

He's looking at me and there's murder in his eyes. I give him a big smile and walk on out the door. I close it softly.

Back in the truck, I sit for a minute, struggling, and then give in to the urge to laugh and soon I'm laughing so hard I can barely remember how to get the truck out onto the road and headed back down the hill to the house. I park right next to the kitchen door, grab the backpack, and put it back into the closet before heading back to the kitchen. I feel like having a drink or two.

The rest of the evening passes in kind of a blur, and I go to sleep on the couch, as usual. When I wake up the next morning it takes me a second to realize that Jerry's standing right in front of me.

"You should lock your door, Boone's Farm Boy," he says.

I don't get up, just pull my knees up to my chest and then kick, hard as I can, with both feet. I'm aiming for his gut but hit a little lower, and the noise he makes is like something out of a bad horror movie. He staggers back and drops to the floor, curled up and sobbing in pain. I get up and go over to him and put my foot on his neck and lean just a little.

When I let up he scrambles to his feet and hobbles out the door. I watch him out the window and when I see him open the trunk and take out a tire iron, I go down the hall to the closet.

When Jerry comes back in I'm standing at the end of the hallway pointing the shotgun at him. He stops dead in his tracks.

"Best thing you can do is leave right now and not come back on this property again," I say.

He starts to raise the tire iron and I work the pump once. He lowers the iron and backs up until his ass runs into the kitchen door. He's fumbling for the knob with his free hand, but he can't find it. I take a step toward him and lower the shotgun until the barrel is pointing at his feet.

"I know you don't like me, and I don't much care one way or the other. You can think whatever you want, but don't make fun of my name and don't come breaking into my house. Next time I'll treat you like anybody that comes in here to rob me." I wave the gun back and forth. "You understand me?"

He nods.

"What are you going to call me, if we see each other again?"

He swallows once. "Boone."

I rest the end of the gun on the floor. "Right. Goodbye, Jerry."

He finds the knob, jerks the door open, and almost falls getting down the steps to his car. He misses the mailbox, but not by much, and cranks the wheel around and heads back up to Gamaliel's house.

I take the shotgun back to the closet and put it back. If I'm going to use that thing, I think to myself, I guess I ought to load it sooner or later. On the way back to the living room I stop by the kitchen and put on some water. With the weather starting to turn colder I'm thinking about coffee in the morning instead of anything cold. Last time I was at the store I bought some instant, and I spoon some into the cup and wait for the water to boil.

I pour the boiling water into the cup, stir it up, and add a little shine to it. When I carry it back into the living room I almost drop it on the floor because I can't stop seeing Daddy on the floor of the barn. I know it's because I picked up the shotgun and I never was really going to shoot Jerry even though he's a genuine asshole, but just having it in my hands brings it all back.

I get a few sips down before I'm sitting on the edge of the couch, my head in my hands, crying like a baby. I cry and cry, loud, part of me glad that I'm alone in the house, mostly I'm just giving in, not even trying to stop.

Chapter Twenty

The coffee is cold by the time I reach for it and I drink it anyway, rinse the cup in the sink, and turn the stove back on to heat the water up again. I spoon in the coffee, add the water and another little bit of shine, and still have the jar out on the counter when there's a knock on the door. After a moment of panic, I slide the jar back into the cabinet, pick up the cup of coffee, and go the the kitchen door.

It's Carrie, and she's furious. I've never seen her like this. I decide not to invite her inside and step out onto the top step. She stands there for a second and then lights into me.

"You had no right to attack my husband, no right at all! He's up there, still in pain, lying on the couch, and I'm thinking about filing charges against you. You hear me, Boone? You want to explain yourself to the police?"

I take a deep breath. You need to be calm right now, I say to myself. She can't go to the police.

"Carrie, I — "

"Mrs. Phillips."

"Sorry. Mrs. Phillips, I don't know what Jerry told you, but when I woke up a while ago, he was in my living room. He came into my house. When I kicked him, I just wanted him to go away. Then when he came back with a tire iron, I — "

"What do you mean, tire iron?"

"Did he not tell you that part? He went out after I kicked him and I looked out the window and he was opening his trunk and then he got out a tire iron and came back into the house."

She's cooling off a little. Still mad, but listening.

"So when he came back in with that in his hand, I was standing in the hallway right back there," I pointed back into the house, "with my daddy's shotgun. I'd appreciate it if you wouldn't tell him this, but it wasn't loaded. I just wanted him to go away and leave me alone."

Carrie shakes her head. "You bluffed him with an empty gun? I don't think I'll tell him that. No, that would not be good."

I look right at her and say, "All I want is to be left alone. I admit it made me mad when he made fun of my name. You can tell Jerry that I don't want any trouble and I won't come looking for it. If it would make things better I can wait to come and visit Gamaliel until after you two go back home."

187

She's looking at me kind of strange. Finally she says, "Have you been crying, Boone? Is everything all right with you?"

I shake my head. "No, no, nothing like that, Mrs. Phillips. Didn't sleep well last night."

She doesn't believe me, I can tell that, but she doesn't push and I'm grateful for that.

"Would you tell Jerry for me that as long as he leaves me alone, I got no reason to fight him at all, and I'd rather we just stay away from each other?"

What I don't say but I hope Gamaliel will is that if they do get the law in this, I might be only a kid, but I'm from around here, and Jerry's a stranger. People around here tend to stick together. If it came down to my word against Jerry's, I think I might be able to get the law to see things my way. He was on my property.

What I don't want is them coming around asking questions about Momma and Daddy. Hannah I can explain away with her visit to her Aunt Claire, but both parents being gone for as long as they have been would be a lot harder.

Carrie is looking at me like I've been talking out loud, which panics me for just a second.

Then she says, "I think once he stops hurting so much he might forget about the filing charges part, but he's not going to want to see you again, Boone."

"I can live with that," I say, and mean every word of it.

She gives me one more look before going back to her car. "Stay down here, Boone. When we're ready to leave I'll come by and let you know. Pop will need somebody to talk to, and I'm guessing so do you." And she was gone.

I go back inside and sit down on the couch. Don't much like how this day is starting out. The house is empty and quiet and I don't want to fill it up with the TV noise. Then I realize it's been way too long since I went up to the pool.

I get up right then and grab a small bottle of shine to take with me, step outside, and lock the door. Nobody to say goodbye to, nobody to wonder where I'm going or to tell me to get back before lunch. I miss Momma a lot sometimes.

The path is grown up some since I haven't been walking it like usual, and I wonder why that is, since right now I got nothing but time. Shrugging it off, I head on up to the pool and sit down in my regular spot.

It doesn't seem right somehow, like something's changed. I look around and, besides the leaves turning and the vines retreating, it all looks the same. The water still fills that deep pool and then runs on out over those two or three little steps, kind of a mini waterfall. I stay for a few more minutes,

189

trying to get the feeling back, and then give up and head back down to the house.

I get there just in time to see the four-wheeler parked right next to the pickup and one of the two guys at the back door. He's looking inside like he's checking the place out; I slip into the barn quiet as I can, put down the jar, and grab the shovel. Then I put it down and grab the pickaxe. Either those guys or their four-wheeler are in some deep shit. Easing the door open, I step out into the yard.

The one still outside doesn't see me until I'm almost on him. Then he yells and jumps on the four-wheeler, trying to get it started, all the time yelling for his buddy still inside. I swing the pickaxe as hard as I can.

The point of the axe clangs off the spare gas can on the back of the luggage rack, and gas starts leaking out on the ground. The guy gets the thing started just as his friend comes running out of the house with the shotgun in his hand. I scream at him and jump toward him, raising the axe over my head. He's standing there waiting on his buddy to swing around and slow down enough for him to jump on. When I charge at him yelling at the top of my lungs, he heads for the barn. His partner is already halfway across the field, getting faster all the time. He cuts left at the barn door, running for his life, Daddy's shotgun in his hand.

With me right behind him, he ducks around the side of the barn and I hear the saplings we have run across the rear opening rattle and know he just climbed over them. I reverse and head back to the front of the barn, getting there just as he is pushing the door open. He sees me and tries to slide through the narrow opening he's made, and he can't get the shotgun through.

I can see the look in his eye. He really wants that gun and he's got about a second to decide how important it is to him. He looks at the pickaxe in my hand, drops the gun, and sprints for the road. I chase him until I get to the road and then watch him go.

When I get back and pick up the gun I realize that part of me wanted him to just take the damn thing and go, get it out of the house, out of my life. Nothing but misery connected to that thing.

But I need it, and I know I do. Living here by myself, especially with Gamaliel's money and shine to protect, I need it. Unless I can think of a better hiding place, one that would be so much trouble that a thief would most likely just go somewhere else. I put the pickaxe back in the barn, pick up the shotgun, and go back to the house, dusting off the gun as I go.

A quick check of the shine and the backpack, and I know that they didn't find out what all was here. If you just look at the place, it looks like there's not

191

much here to steal. I'm hoping that's the way the guy saw it; maybe when he hooks back up with his partner he'll tell him it's not worth worrying about.

This day just keeps getting worse and worse.

Chapter Twenty-One

I manage to make it through lunch without any more visitors, and I'm starting to think about that better hiding place. I need someplace to put Gamaliel's stash and our shine that would be hard to find or hard to get to or both. And then it comes to me. I go into the kitchen and rummage through all the drawers and come up empty, so I head for the grocery store. I need a few things anyway.

When I get back, I put the cheese and meat in the refrigerator and the canned stuff on the shelves. The bread and the cereal I just leave out on the counter. Then I go into the closet and get the backpack.

The two boxes are about the same size, and I don't have to worry about the pistol anymore, which is good. I take the box with the silver dollars in it and open up the box of ziplock bags and pull one out and slide the box inside. I push all the air I can out of it and zip it closed. It takes a couple of tries. Then I get another bag and put all that inside it, and then do it one more time. I get out the roll of duct tape and wrap around and around until it's covered, and then put the whole mess into another ziplock. It's still pretty small, thicker than my history textbook but not as long or wide.

I repeat the process with the other box and then check the time. Early afternoon; plenty of time. I head out of the house with both boxes in my backpack and go back up to the pool.

I stop half a dozen times along the way and just stand there, listening. No noise besides what is supposed to be there. No leaves rustling or branches breaking, and I don't see any sign of anybody but me having been here.

The water is cold, colder than I remember it being, when I step into the pool and wade out to the center, the boxes tucked under one arm, the other one extended for balance. There's a place I know across from where I usually sit, where the rocks pile up to a little higher than the water's edge. The brush, thick and almost waist high, grows right up to the pool's edge on that side. When I reach the pile of rocks I can barely stretch over them to a place just above the waterline, a place big enough to set the boxes while I work.

It works better than I hoped it would; when I take the top three rocks off the pile and set them aside, there's a small empty space behind them. Removing a few more rocks enlarges the hole to just big enough to hold both boxes. When I slide them in, just above the surface of the water, there's enough room to put one of the smaller rocks in front of them, and when the three go back on top, the boxes are completely invisible. I put the extra rocks along the edge and wade back to the spot where I usually sit. Getting out, I massage my calves and feet while I examine my handiwork.

I can barely tell that the rocks have been moved, and I know exactly where to look. Nice job, Boone, I say to myself. Nice job.

When I'm almost back to the house, I think I see movement. Slowing down, I move forward as quietly as I can. When I get to the edge of the woods I can see somebody walking around the house, looking in windows. For a second I wish I had Gamaliel's pistol with me, but I decide to step out and show myself when it's clear that it's only one person. The front yard is partially hidden from view, so I can't see a vehicle of any kind. Nothing but the old pickup truck.

I'm standing out in the open when the person rounds the corner after making a complete circuit of the house. When Nancy sees me she looks startled and a little guilty, like she's been caught doing something she isn't supposed to be doing. Which is true, I guess, since she was sneaking around my house peeping in the windows.

She still looks flustered and is standing, shifting her weight back and forth from one foot to the other, like she's trying to decide whether to come toward me or retreat to her car, which I'm guessing is around at the front of the house. I take a step towards her and say, "Looking for me?"

She grins a little, embarrassed, and says, "How are you, Boone? Haven't seen you at school for a while."

"No, I guess you haven't," I reply. "I'm so far behind now I don't see much use in it. Besides, I've been busy."

"Listen, I'm sorry I was sneaking around like that, you must think I'm some kind of pervert or something," Nancy still looks like she'd been caught shoplifting a candy bar or something. I'd never seen her this uncomfortable.

"It's okay, really," I say, "You want to come inside?"

The last time I tried to get her to come in she wouldn't do it when she found out nobody else was home. I'm trying to decide whether or not to mention that I'm still here by myself when she says, "Why are your pants legs so wet?"

I look down and then back up to Nancy's face. "I was up at the pool and thought I'd try a new place to sit and listen to the water. Slipped on the way and slid in. No big deal, I guess I'll stick to my old spot. So you want to come in? I need to warm up a little."

"Sure."

Well, I think to myself. This might be the first time anybody's come to see me since I lost my whole family. Carrie and Jerry stopping by without getting out of their car doesn't count, and I don't count Jerry's early morning visit, when he ended up running away from my shotgun, as anything either. At least anything I want to remember.

I go up to the kitchen door and open it, step inside, and hold it open for Nancy to come in. She takes a couple of steps in, looks around, and starts laughing. I look at the kitchen and don't see anything out of the ordinary. When I look at her, she's shaking her head, looking at me, and finally sweeps her arm around the room.

"You can tell a single guy lives here, Boone," she says. I give her a look, but she's not being mean about it, at least I don't think so.

"What's wrong with it?" I say, trying not to sound angry or defensive.

"Nothing's wrong with it," she says, "it's just that a woman would never let her kitchen get like this."

I look around again, don't see anything wrong, and look back at her helplessly.

"Never mind," she says. "So what have you been busy doing?"

So I tell her about Mr. Everett being in the hospital and me taking care of his place, and she nods and says, "I know, or rather my parents know him. He kind of keeps to himself, doesn't he?"

"Yeah, I guess the only reason I know him as well as I do is because we live so close."

"So do you need to go check on him this afternoon?"

"No," I say, "his daughter and her husband are staying with him right now. I think they're leaving tomorrow or the next day, but right now they don't need me to check on him. Besides, he's a tough old man, probably doesn't need anybody all over him like a mother hen."

"Maybe he just likes company, Boone. Everybody likes a little company now and then."

She's still standing in the middle of the kitchen. I say, "I'm sorry, Nancy, forgetting my manners. You want to go sit in the living room?"

She smiles. "Thought you were going to make me stand in the kitchen the whole time."

Now it's my turn to be embarrassed. I wave her toward the living room and she goes in ahead of me. When she sees it she doesn't laugh, but she does look at me a little strange.

"You just have the couch and the TV? Most people have more furniture than this." She looks at the couch; it still has a pillow on it from last night when I slept there. I walk over and pick it up and say, "Fell asleep on the couch last night, watching TV."

She looks a little uncertain, but when I sit down on the couch, all the way out on the end, she takes the other end and we sit in silence for a long two minutes.

Finally she says, "So you're not coming back to school?"

I shake my head. "Not sure, but I'm not seeing much use in it right now."

"Did you hear about Mr. Timmons?"

"No," I shake my head, "I don't watch the news much. Something happen already?"

"My parents say he's in a lot of trouble, more than he'll ever be able to talk his way out of. They say some of the students have pictures from some of those parties at his house, and one of them, a guy named Curt, I can't think of his last name, is giving the police a lot of names and dates to keep himself out of trouble. Mr. Timmons might go to jail for a long time, that's what they are all saying."

So, Curt is a snitch. I am not a bit surprised. But I really don't care about Mr. Timmons or Curt or any of that. I'm thinking that I have a girl in my house, for the very first time, and I'm thinking Nancy is really good looking. She catches me looking at her all up and down and blushes. Before she can say anything or get up and leave, I say, "Listen, Nancy, I've been thinking about getting a dog. You remember the name of that guy, I think he was one year behind us, who used to come to school saying that his dog had a new litter of puppies and he was going to have to give them away?"

She looks at the floor, thinking. Then she looks at me. "Gary, I think, but I can't think of his last name. He lives over close to us, just a little farther down towards Knoxville. I haven't heard him talk about puppies anytime lately, but I'll ask him if you want me to."

"That'd be great," I say, "I'd appreciate it."

"Want me to call you when I hear something?"

"You can call me anytime." The words are out before I have a chance to think about them, and I say to myself, what a stupid thing to say. Like a bad movie or TV show. I look at the floor, afraid that if I look up I'll see her laughing at me.

"Really, Boone? Cause you never call me, and I don't know whether or not you even want to talk to me."

Chapter Twenty-Two

She's not laughing at me. When I look at her she looks kind of scared, or uncertain, or something, I don't know what, so I do the only thing I can think of to do. I slide over and put my arm around her. When I give her shoulders a hug she turns sideways and we're hugging for real, there on the couch, and then I look down at her face and her eyes are closed and her face is tilted up to me and I've never kissed anybody before, not counting Momma and Hannah, and those were on the cheek. Her lips are just barely apart and I lean down and touch mine to hers.

She jerks her head back and I say, "Sorry, sorry," and she's up on her feet but she doesn't go anywhere.

"I . . I . . I think I should go," she says, like she's out of breath, and I nod and say, "I understand. Listen, I'm really sorry."

"No," she shakes her head, "don't be sorry, I just better get out of here, okay?"

I nod and stand up and she moves toward the door. I follow her out into the yard and when we get to her car she turns and puts her arms around my neck and pulls my head down to hers and gives me a kiss right on the lips, so soft, and then she says, "You be sure and call me."

I watch her leave, a little shaky, feeling like I need to sit down, so I head back to the house and pour a strong S&S and sit back on the couch.

She wants me to call her. I need to be sure and do that. When do I do that? Do I give her time to get home? What if she's not going straight home? Do I wait until tomorrow? I really don't know what I'm doing here, totally lost, and even if Daddy was still around he wouldn't be any help, he'd just tell me to take her and not worry about her saying no. I saw the way he treated Momma and I don't want that to be how I do things.

I could ask Gamaliel, he would help me out, but I can't because that asshole Jerry is still up there. Wonder what Jerry would tell me to do? The thought of asking him makes me laugh out loud. I don't know many grown men less mature than me but I'm thinking he's one that is.

I decide to call her tomorrow. Tonight doesn't feel right somehow, and I'm ready for some TV and, well, nothing. It doesn't often bother me that since I dropped out of school I don't do much of anything, but tonight it does. Maybe I'll think about what Nancy said, about that guy's name being Gary something. If I can remember his name I could see if he is in the phone book and give him a call. Don't know whether he would remember me or not but I'm thinking with what's going on with me right now a big mean dog is just what I need.

Harrington. Gary Harrington. It takes me most of the evening and his name doesn't really come to me until I stop thinking about it, give up, and turn on the TV. I'm sure that's right, though, I can see him coming up to me in the hallway, "Hey, Boone, you know anybody that wants a dog? I've got some new puppies, gotta get rid of them, let me know." When was the last time he did that? End of last year?

Yeah, I think it was. Maybe his bitch is ready for more puppies. I don't get the feeling that he keeps her up when she's in heat, so whatever is mixed with Rottweiler is a crapshoot, but if it's like last time the price will be right.

I find two Harringtons in the phone book. One lives out on Mine Road, on a different side of Knoxville from where I am, so, because of what Nancy said, I take a chance and call the other one.

It turns out to be a good guess, and Gary's dog had pups about 10 or 12 weeks ago. "They're all gone, dude, all but the runt. She's the only one I've got left, and Dad's getting ready to drop her by the side of the road or into the river, so if you want her she's yours."

I tell him I'll take her and by the next evening I've got a dog.

She's a pitiful thing, definitely a runt, but she's all over me as soon as I get her from Gary and I'm real glad I saved her from the river.

It's another week before I decide on a name. She gets used to the place almost immediately, running all over the house, chewing on everything just like a puppy is supposed to do, and I finally decide to call her Frankie.

I think about my brother almost every day, and, even though it's a girl dog, I think the name fits, and it's nice to have Frankie around again.

"Someday I'll tell you about where you got your name, Frankie," I say to her, and she looks up at me like she understands every word. What I don't understand is why I didn't get a dog a long time ago. All those weepy commercials about dogs and love and loyalty and all that stuff, damned if they're not right.

Frankie and I are out in the yard a couple of days later when Carrie and Jerry pull up into the yard. I scoop Frankie up into my arms and go over to Carrie's side and she rolls down her window.

"Nice dog," she says, and reaches out to scratch Frankie behind the ear. Frankie's really eating this up until Jerry leans close to Carrie to say something and Frankie starts growling her little puppy growl. I can't help it; I laugh out loud, and I swear I see a smile on Carrie's face. Jerry jerks back to his side and says, "Let's get this over with."

"We're going on back home now, Boone," she says, trying to keep a straight face. "You take good care of Pop, you hear?"

"Yes, ma'am," I say. "Me and Frankie, we'll look after him."

Jerry snorts but doesn't say anything. Carrie rolls up the window and they back out and they're gone. Then they pull back in and Carrie motions me over. She hands me a slip of paper.

"Our phone number," she says. "In case you or Pop need anything."

"Thanks," I say, and this time they really do leave.

Only had her a little while, and I can't believe how big Frankie is. From the runt of the litter she's growing like crazy; already getting harder to pick up and eating everything in sight. Momma sent me another fifty a couple of weeks ago, but money's getting really tight, and I know it's just going to keep getting more expensive. Plus in her last letter, a really short note, she said that Jake didn't like her sending money through the mail and she might not be able to get me any more. Poor Momma.

I take Frankie up to Gamaliel's house and she loves that old man, almost as much as she loves me. I think he likes having her around; he's even talked to me about getting a dog for himself.

"What do you think, Boone, maybe one of those half-dog, half-wolf beasts?" he'd say, scratching Frankie behind the ears. "He'd make a morning snack out of this little girl."

Gamaliel's doing okay, I guess, but he looks thin to me. I'm no good as a cook, so all I can do for him is fry up some fish or one of those pre-formed hamburgers, and he's getting to the point where he won't even finish one of them. When I try to get him to eat more he gets testy and I've gradually stopped pushing him. I figure that's Carrie's job anyway. I'm just supposed to look in on him.

He asked for one of the gallons of shine back when I came up the first time after Carrie and Jerry had left, but he's drinking that gallon real slow and hasn't mentioned the money or the silver dollars since he got back from the hospital. I think about mentioning it, but then I think maybe I'll just keep quiet about it. Maybe he's forgotten about it. As soon as I say that to myself I know it's bullshit; the old guy is way too sharp for that.

One day he and I are in the sunroom, Frankie between us on the floor, we're just sipping and talking, and he says, "About that money . . . ."

I put down my glass and he puts down his.

"Here's what I want you to do, Boone," he says, and he's more serious than I've ever seen him.

"Carrie doesn't know about the money; she does know about the silver dollars, she used to play with them when she was a little girl. I hope you've got both boxes hidden away somewhere where nobody can find them, but what I want you to do, after I'm gone, is to give that box of silver dollars to Carrie and keep your mouth shut about the other box."

"Gamaliel, you know you're going to outlive me," I say, a little unsteady. "You're too mean to die."

He laughs. "Thanks for that, boy. I want you to promise me that you'll do just what I said. I love my daughter, but that Jerry is just an ass, and I don't want him knowing about that other box. He'd be all over that, might even do me in to get it. So you promise me, Boone."

He's looking at me, waiting.

"I promise, Gamaliel," I say solemnly.

"Good," he says. "Pour me another one."

Chapter Twenty-Three

So I do, and one for me, and we sit for a while longer before Frankie and I go back home.

The next day I realize that Nancy hasn't met Frankie yet. As a matter of fact, she hasn't been back or called since that moment on the couch. I look around until I find the piece of paper I have her number on and put it next to the phone. I'll call her tonight, I tell myself.

After six I figure it's late enough and I give her a call.

"Hello?"

I don't recognize the voice, and I realize I don't know anything about her family. Is this her brother, uncle, father?

"Uh, can I speak to Nancy, please?"

"She's doing her homework right now. Can I tell her who called?"

Should I tell them my name? What has she told them about me? I hate having to worry about this kind of shit, but it comes to me and before I even notice it it's there and messing with me. I clear my throat.

"This is Boone, I'm a friend of hers from school."

I hear some talking in the background. Then the same voice is back on the line.

"You should give her another half hour at least to finish up before you try again. I'll tell her you called." There was a pause. "You sure this isn't Randy? You sound like Randy to me. You know she doesn't want anything to do with you."

Now I'm really not sure what to say.

"Uh, no, I mean, I don't even know a Randy. This is Boone. Tell you what, I'll try again in an hour or so."

"Okay, Randy, whatever you say. But I'm telling you she doesn't want to see you anymore, not after last week."

Then he hangs up.

I stand there with the phone in my hand for a second, then put it down.

A half hour goes by, then an hour, and I'm about to pick up the phone when it rings.

"Hello?"

"Boone? It's Nancy."

I breathe a long breath. She sounds good. Better than I remember. That feeling lasts about ten seconds.

"Cyrus told me that you called pretending to be Randy. How do you know about Randy? What has everybody been saying?"

I don't know what to say, but I don't get a chance to say anything.

"You seemed like a nice guy but you're just like all the rest of them. I'm telling you like I told them nothing happened, no matter what Randy is telling people. I'm surprised at you, Boone, that you would be part of this. How could you be such a jerk?"

I try to break in. "Nancy, listen for a second — "

"Why should I listen to you after you playing such a dirty trick on Cyrus?"

She stops for a second and I jump in.

"Nancy, I have no idea who Randy is or what you're talking about. Cyrus or whoever I talked to when I called earlier told me he thought I was Randy, whoever that is, pretending to be Boone. I don't know what this is all about, I just called to talk to you. Maybe you should talk to Cyrus and call me back. Or not." I hang up the phone.

What the hell was that all about? I'm mad and I don't know who to be mad at. Whoever this Cyrus is, he's definitely an asshole, Randy sounds like a real jerk too, and I don't like the way Nancy was talking to me. Not at all. I go into the living room and Frankie's in there, curled up on the blanket that I put down for her next to the couch. Funny, she

210

doesn't like to be up on the couch, but she wants to be close by all the time. She's turning into a really good dog.

"What do you think, Frankie? Does this make any sense to you?"

She thumps her tail on the floor.

"I know, girl, I feel the same way. You and me, right? The hell with the rest of them. Well, there's Gamaliel, he's okay, right?"

When she hears the old guy's name, she's on her feet, like, "Let's go, let's go see him right now!"

I laugh at her and give her a scratch. "You're a good girl, Frankie."

The phone rings.

I look at the little screen. It's Nancy.

I let it ring once more while I try to decide whether or not to pick it up. Before the next ring I grab it.

"Yeah."

"Boone? It's Nancy."

"I saw that on the caller ID thing."

There's a silence.

"Listen, Boone, my little brother's a jerk, okay? I had to back him into a corner and threaten to hurt him before he told me what he did."

I had to smile at that one. Cyrus sounded like he probably wasn't that much younger than Nancy, and the thought of her backing him into a corner was

211

kind of funny and exciting at the same time. I almost said that I wish I could have been there to see that, but I don't.

"I don't know Cyrus."

"You don't want to, believe me. He's two years younger than me, thinks he's all grown up, and then does this stupid kid's stuff to prove he's nowhere near grown up. I thought about making him call you and apologize himself, but then I thought it would be fake and I wasn't sure I wanted him on the phone with you again. So how are you? I thought I'd hear from you before this. Everything okay?"

And already I'm not mad anymore. Not at her, or Cyrus. Maybe at this Randy person, wonder what he did, or tried to do, to Nancy? I think about asking her and decide not to. Maybe when I see her again.

"Yeah, everything's good. The old man's doing pretty well, I'm all right, and I've got something I'd like to show you the next time you're over here."

There's a pause, and then, "Well, I have to stay close to home these days, after what happened with Randy."

I feel a flare of anger, but I try to sound casual. "Sorry, Nancy, I don't know what you're talking about."

"I can't tell you about it, Boone, it was just awful. I mean, nothing bad happened, not really, but he's such a jerk, and he wouldn't take no for an answer."

Now the anger is white-hot inside me. I say, "Did this asshole hurt you? Did he, Nancy?"

She laughs, kind of a small, nervous laugh. "You should watch your language, Boone, but no, he didn't hurt me. Fact is, I may have hurt him a little when I kicked him. At least I hope I did."

"Good for you, girl," I say. She knows how to fight back, I'm thinking. Not like Momma. Momma never fought back. Not that I saw. For a second I wonder what things would have been like if she had, early on. Wouldn't have saved Frankie, nothing would have saved him, but might have been better for me and Hannah and sure as hell would have been better for her. Daddy might have left early on, but that might have been okay, too.

"Boone? Are you still there?"

I realize I'm still holding the phone and Nancy is still on the other end. Wonder how long I've been quiet?

"Yeah, I'm still here. Sorry."

She goes on. "Anyway, I'm staying close to home for a while anyway. You could come over, bring whatever it is you want to show me, Mom could fix dinner."

"I can't do that, Nancy. Bring what I've got to show you to you, I mean."

"Now I'm interested. Wish I could come over and see this big mystery thing. You could still come over here, though."

Now I'm standing here thinking, I've been wearing the same two pairs of jeans for a long time now, and just tee shirts and sweats. I don't have any clean clothes and haven't for a long time.

"Maybe some other time, Nancy. I really can't do it right now."

"Oh, okay." She sounds really disappointed, and I realize that I am too. I'd like to see her.

"Listen, can I get a rain check? I'd like to see you, for real."

I'm not sure what a rain check is, but I read it in a book once and I think it means that I'd like to go, I can't, but I'd like to go later if that's okay.

Nancy laughs. "I didn't know you knew that expression, Boone. Of course you can have a rain check. Call me when you have some time to come over. I'll call you when things change and I feel like I can get out of here."

Another flash of anger, and I think, I really need to keep that shit under control. For a second I'm mad at Nancy because I think she thinks I'm stupid. Then it passes and I say, "Sounds good to me, Nancy, I'll give you a call sometime soon. And tell Cyrus, well, tell him if he's trying to take care of his sister that's one thing, but if he was jerking me around to not ever do that again. Okay?"

"Okay, Boone, I'll talk to you soon, I hope. I'm kind of curious about whatever it is you want to show me."

I hang up and go outside, out to the barn. A quick check shows the shine is still right where I left it, and I'm not worried about the boxes, especially since that conversation with Gamaliel. I decide to make a quick trip up to the pool tomorrow, and maybe swing around to have a look at the still. Not too worried about that, either, since it's been there for who knows how long without being bothered.

Chapter Twenty-Four

The next day I go up to the pond; nothing has changed, no sign of anybody disturbing anything, the branch I left stuck between two of the rocks is still right where I left it. I circle around to the still and find it pretty much as I left it. It looks a little more exposed now that most of the leaves have dropped, and I make a note to ask Gamaliel about that when I go by to see him. I'm wondering if he and Daddy covered it with brush between times they used it or just left it and took a chance that nobody would come by. I know the Thompsons have "No Hunting" and "No Trespassing" signs all over the boundaries of their land and I'm thinking that makes the location of the still a good one. I know Mrs. Thompson patrols her land on that four-wheeler pretty frequently, and everybody else knows that too.

I make the big circle around the pool, stepping over the creek at a narrowing just on our side of the fence, and make my way over to the Everett place. I usually drive the truck up to see Gamaliel, but I thought since I was out anyway I'd cut through the woods and come in from behind the shed. It's the path, if you could call it a path, that Gamaliel took to the still back when he was talking me through the last few steps before we took the shine down to his place to filter it. I smile thinking about that, about getting to know the old guy, and how good it is to have a neighbor like him.

I don't even notice how close I am to his tool shed until I hear the pistol and think, what the hell's going on out here? The stinging in my arm is there before I hear the next shot, and I look down at the blood and it seems like there's a lot of it and I realize I'm still hearing shots. I hit the ground and scramble around behind a tree, waiting until things calm down before I move. I hear the four-wheeler start up and then I'm up and running and shouting, "Gamaliel! It's me, Boone! Don't shoot!"

By the time I round the shed the four-wheeler is headed across the field onto the Thompson's land, and I can see broken glass and it looks like the door's hanging wrong in the doorway. I step out into the yard and I hear the old man's voice. "I don't know who you are, but one more step and I'll drop you where you stand!"

I stand still, pressing my hand against my upper arm; I'm starting to feel a little sick and I call out,

"Gamaliel, it's me, Boone, I just came through the woods and saw the four-wheeler take off across the field. Are you okay?"

After a couple of seconds I see his head peeking up through the bottom of the shattered window to the right of the door.

"Boone? Did you say Boone?"

"Yeah, it's me. I'm shot. I need to come in and let you look at it. Okay?"

"Oh, hell, Boone, was it me that shot you? You come on in here. I think you need to look at me too. I'm not feeling so good."

I come up slow and can't get through the back door the way it's hanging, so I say, "I need to go around and come in the front, Gamaliel. I'll be right there."

"You might want to hurry, boy." He sounds weak.

I hustle around to the front and into the house, down the hall, and into the sunroom. It's a mess, and so is Gamaliel.

He's sitting on the floor, looking around, and there's blood on the floor but not a lot. When I see that I feel a little better, and I go over to him and say, "Can I help you up, you need to get up so I can see what's going on here."

"I'm not sure I can get up right now," he answers.

I can't see any place he's bleeding, so I put my hand on his shoulder and he pulls away from me.

218

"Dammit, Boone, that hurt."

"Sorry," I say. Never mind how much I'm hurting here.

"What the hell happened, man?"

He shakes his head, slow, like it's his neck or his back. "I don't know where they came from. I was sitting in my chair, like I do every day, and then I came into the kitchen to refill my glass, and when I came back I just got set back down and I hear this godawful noise, and then the glass is breaking, and they're trying to come inside."

"Who's trying to come inside?"

"Couple of young thugs, is all I know. I sure am glad I got that pistol back from you. They didn't expect that at all, I could tell. First shot finished breaking out the window, and then they leave the door half off its hinges and start trying to get away, and I jump up so I can get another shot off and I trip on something, I don't know what, and I fall into the broken glass right when the gun goes off again, and I might've fired one more time, I'm not sure, and then they were gone on that four wheeled machine of theirs. That's when I heard you hollering at me."

I breathe a long breath. "So you didn't get shot? You're all right?"

He tries to stand up and makes it, but just barely. He sways back and forth a little and then gets his balance. "I think so. Probably pulled a muscle or three, but I'm all right. But you're not." He points to my arm. "Dammit, Boone, I did that, didn't I? I am so sorry, Boone, I'm so sorry."

I try to wave it off but that's not happening. Finally I sit down on the chair I usually sit in and say, "I don't think it's bad, it just hurts like hell."

"You let me take a look at that," he says and starts toward me and almost falls down. We look at each other and both of us start laughing and pretty soon we're out of breath and can't even talk we're laughing so hard.

I get my breath back first. "You can't even walk across the room, and you're going to fix my arm?"

"Damn right I am. Just let me get there and I'll show you."

Which sets us off again, but not as long this time.

I lean forward and slip off my tee shirt and twist around to look at my upper arm. There's a gash about three inches down from my shoulder, not deep, but bleeding like a stuck pig. I look over at Gamaliel and say, "I need something to wash this out with and a gauze bandage, and I think I'll be okay. You got any of that stuff?"

He nods and points to the kitchen. "Up on the top shelf, cabinet to the left of the stove," he says. "Might as well bring it all over here. It's in a box. I need some fixing up too." He grimaces. "I think mine are mostly strains and pulls and shit like that, just a few cuts from the glass when I fell in it."

We start fixing each other and ourselves up and pretty soon all the bleeding is stopped and we sit facing each other and just look at each other for a time.

"Those guys came around my place a while back," I say finally.

"Did you get a good look at either one of them?"

I shake my head. "One was inside and I thought I was going to get a piece of him, but he outran me. The other one was on the four-wheeler and I didn't have a chance to get a good look."

He nods and I continue, "What about today? You get any kind of look at them?"

He shakes his head.

"So now what?" I say, looking around at the mess. "Call the law?"

Gamaliel shakes his head and then winces. "No, no law, what are they going to do? Nothing missing, a little property damage, no descriptions worth a damn. Anyway, since they got shot at here I don't think they'll be back. Thieves go for the easy ones usually."

I am absolutely fine with that. This situation isn't going to get any better with the law coming into it; they don't know us, we don't trust them, it's a guaranteed failure all around.

"I need a drink," he says, and since I feel the same way and I'm not as banged up as he is, I offer to go into the kitchen and mix a couple.

"What are you having?" I say over my shoulder as I'm heading into the kitchen.

"Shine and a couple of ice cubes," he says.

I decide to have the same and we sit and drink and tell each other how our wounds are worse than the other's. I get the best line, though.

"At least I didn't shoot you, Gamaliel. You can't say the same about me."

He looks so pitiful that for a minute I'm sorry I said it, and then he says, "I'm not worried. You couldn't have hit me if you tried."

I go on back home and check on Frankie. She's good, and everything seems to be in order. Well, I think to myself, if he's right about thieves usually picking easy targets, both of us should be okay. At least I hope so.

Chapter Twenty-Five

A couple of days later I decide to call Nancy again. Before I do, I gather up all the clothes I have and head into town. I've never been to a laundromat before, and I wouldn't go now if I could make the washing machine work. I try pushing and pulling and turning every knob I see and I can't get water to start filling the tub. I check out the dryer; it's a lot older than the washer, but it looks like it's going to run all right, so all I have to do is wash and then bring everything home. It's a good thing I end up there at the same time as a woman doing her family's clothes; she saw me loading the washer and came over.

"You might want to split that into two loads," she says, "and put all those tee shirts and underwear together."

"Thanks," I say.

"Your momma usually does this, right?"

"Can't get the washer to work. Dryer's fine." I am in no mood to talk to this person. This whole thing just reminds me that Momma's not around to take care of this kind of stuff. So I end up being mad at the woman trying to help me and mad at Momma and mad at myself for not knowing how to wash my own clothes.

The clothes are really heavy when they're wet, and I almost drop them on the ground outside the kitchen door, but I manage to get them inside and put part of them in the dryer. It takes a couple of hours but eventually I get everything dry and throw it all on my bed. Now if Nancy invites me over I'll have clean clothes.

When I call her she doesn't mention me coming over. I'm more disappointed than I thought I would be. The thought of eating a real meal and talking to people is something I miss a lot, I guess, even though I don't think about it much.

"So what have you been up to?"

I start to tell her about the guys trying to break into Gamaliel's house and about him shooting me by accident but catch myself in time. At the same time I think I won't try too hard to get her over here, at least until my arm heals. I don't want to have to explain that.

That makes me think I should call Carrie and tell her about Gamaliel, but I know that if I did that without talking to him he'd be furious. Couldn't really blame him for that, either, I'd feel the same way.

So I say, "Not much. How about you?"

She tells me about school and how the whole place has turned on Mr. Timmons and how the seniors that used to be such hot stuff are slinking around the halls and trying to be invisible. She and most of the other students are loving every minute of it. I start to ask about Randy and decide not to; no reason to start that up again.

"So when am I going to get to see this surprise you talked about last time?"

I'm surprised. It sounds like Nancy is kind of inviting herself over. Just to make sure, I say, "Well, it's not the kind of thing I can just put in my pocket and meet you somewhere."

"That's okay," she says, "I could drop by sometime after school."

"That's good," I say, uncomfortable all of a sudden. "I mean that you're getting out again and all."

I'm thinking back to the last time she was over here, and how quick she wanted out right after we kissed and then how she kissed me goodby at her car before she took off. I mean, I really want her to come back over and stay a while this time. I'm just scared, I guess.

Oh, well. What the hell. "I still have it, the surprise, I mean."

She's quiet for a second and then says, "I might come by next week sometime, if that'd be okay with you."

"You bet," I say, not caring whether it sounds stupid or not.

"Okay, then," she says, and I know I'm supposed to say something and I don't know what that is. Then I think of something.

"Just call me before so I'll be sure and be home."

"I will," she says. "Goodbye, Boone."

Now the time is dragging, because I'm waiting for Nancy to call and I'm waiting for those assholes on the four-wheeler to come back around and I'm waiting for Gamaliel to get better so I won't feel bad about not calling Carrie.

I go up and see the old man every day and he looks okay, like he's going to get over the fall. I do most of the work putting glass back in the windows and fixing the door; it's coming on winter and he needs the house sealed up. He fusses about my arm but it really was not much more than a scratch. It'll leave a scar, though, which none of the other guys have, so that's cool. Or it would be if I ever saw anybody.

I think about how that would go. I'd pull my tee shirt off to jump in the lake or get ready for gym class and somebody would say, "Where'd you get the scar, Boone? Fall off your tricycle again?"

Everybody would laugh, and then I'd say, "Nah, I didn't fall. Bullet just grazed me. No big deal."

Then I'd just glance around the room once, shrug my shoulders, and go on with whatever I was doing. And if anybody said that I was making it all up, I'd just give them a look, and they'd know I wasn't lying. Getting shot'll do that to a guy. Give him that look, that he can use whenever he needs to.

This time when I knock on the Gamaliel's door there's no answer. I try again, and then head around to the back. When I get to the corner of the house and can see around back I want to go back to about five minutes ago.

He's laying on the ground at the bottom of the steps that go from the back door down to the path that leads to the shed. I stand there for a second and then run over to him and bend down next to his head. He's not breathing.

I hit him as hard as I can on the back, screaming, "Don't you dare die on me, you old bastard! Don't you dare!"

Then, like a miracle right in front of me, he moves a little. He tries to push himself up off the ground and I hold him down.

"Don't move, Gamaliel, I'm going to call the doctor and Carrie."

Shaking his head, he tries to get up again. I let him try and he gives it his best, but can't straighten his arms. Falling back down to the ground, he nods. "Guarrr butt."

His voice is so weak, I can barely hear him and I'm right next to him.

"Don't go anywhere," I say, and he grins, but it's a feeble, pitiful thing.

"Iwo," he says.

Chapter Twenty-Six

I haven't been in a hospital since before Frankie died. First minute in, and already I don't like it.

There's a guy at a big desk and I go up to him.

"Where's Gamaliel?"

He looks at me like I'm an idiot.

"I said — "

"Yes, sir, I heard you," he says. "Name?"

"Gamaliel Everett."

"Are you a relative?"

I shake my head. "Neighbor."

Now it's his turn to shake his head. "I'm sorry, Mr. ?"

"My name's Boone. Why are you sorry?"

"Only relatives allowed in ICU. You can go to the waiting area and check with his family there if you like."

I take a deep breath. "You don't understand, I'm like family to him, he's my neighbor."

He's saying no before I get all the words out, and that really pisses me off. I take two steps back, wondering if I can clear the desk and land right in his lap. The look in his eyes is almost funny; it's like he knows what I'm thinking about doing. He pushes his chair back and stands up.

"Sir, I'm going to have to ask you to leave." He makes some kind of motion with his hand and I see movement in the corner of my eye. I turn my head just enough to see the policeman walking toward us, and I decide not to jump this guy. Even though he deserves it.

"I don't want any trouble here, if you'll just tell me where this waiting room is I'll get out of your way."

"Well . . . ." he says slowly. The policeman is standing beside me now. I look over and smile at him; he doesn't smile back.

"Please, sir, he means an awful lot to me. I can talk to Carrie, that's his daughter, I'll bet she's up there right now."

He looks down at a clipboard that's sitting on his desk, then he nods at the policeman. "Carrie is listed here as Mr. Everett's daughter."

The policeman puts a hand on my shoulder and I try not to react.

"Why don't I walk with you? I'll show you where the room is."

"I'd appreciate that, sir, I really would."

He stays close the whole way, but he doesn't put his hand on me again. When we get to the room, Carrie and her husband are both sitting next to the window; Carrie gets up as soon as she sees me. Jerry glances at me and goes back to his magazine.

She comes over to me and gives me a hug. The policeman shrugs and walks off.

"Thank you, Boone, thank you so much for what you did," she says, and her voice is unsteady.

"I didn't really do anything, ma'am," I say. I'm pretty uncomfortable with this whole thing.

"Nonsense," she says firmly. "Who knows how long he would have been out there on the ground if you hadn't come to check on him."

"I guess so," I say, hoping she'll stop this soon. "How is the old man doing?"

Jerry looks up from his magazine. "A little respect there, boy."

Carrie ignores him. "He's still asleep. They want him to get as much rest as he can. They say he was dehydrated and his blood alcohol was very high." She looks at me. "You know anything about that, Boone?"

"You know I can't buy anything, you said so yourself," I answer, looking around the room. "No store'd sell me anything."

I can feel her eyes on me.

"When can I go in and see him?" I really want us to talk about something else, anything else.

She looks at me for another second and then decides to drop it. "I don't know, Boone, they won't even let me in for more than a minute or two. Jerry can't even go in with me, so I'm thinking it'll be a while.

"I want you to look after the place while he's in here, okay? Just go by every day or so and make sure the place is still locked up, you know, like that." She looks and sounds worried.

"Sure," I say. "I'll be glad to."

"How was he the last time you saw him?"

"Good, he was good."

"When was that, do you remember which day it was?"

"Two days ago, I think. Yeah, it was early afternoon, two days ago. I just stayed for a little while."

"And everything was okay? Pop was all right when you left?"

"Yeah, fine. Just like usual." Not like he was a week or so ago, I think to myself. But she didn't ask about that. This whole conversation is starting to bother me. I guess she must have sensed something.

"Boone, are you sure everything was okay with Pop? Sometimes he doesn't tell me stuff, and I'm counting on you to let me know what's going on with him."

"Everything was fine, like I said, it was early afternoon, a couple of days ago, we sat and talked for a while. Nothing going on."

"Okay," I can tell she doesn't believe me. Now I just want to leave.

"I'm coming back tomorrow to check on him, okay?"

Carrie nods. I can see she's worried about the old guy. Truth is, so am I.

When I get home I stand in the kitchen for a second and then pour a good drink of the triple filtered shine. No S&S this time, no ice, just the pure stuff. I take it with me into the living room, turn around once real slow, and then head out into the yard. It's a little cold, but I make the trip up to the pool anyway, sit on my rock, and sip it slow and think about Gamaliel. I have a bad feeling about this.

When I get back to the house I'm not inside for more than a minute when the phone rings. I pick it up expecting it to be Carrie giving me bad news from the hospital, but it's not.

"Hello, is this Boone?"

"Yeah, who's this?"

"This is your aunt Claire. How are you, Boone?"

What I want to do is throw the phone. She hasn't called me in years, and since she took Momma and Hannah in, I haven't heard a word from her about how are you, come see us, need a place to stay, kiss my ass, anything. I just stand there with the phone to my ear, trying not to scream at her and smash the phone.

"Boone, are you there? Have you seen your mother? She left to go shopping with Jake, that guy she took up with, and that's been three days and we haven't seen her or heard from her. We're getting worried and I don't know what to tell Hannah."

"Why are you calling me?"

"Don't take that tone with me, young man. I'm trying to help here." She gets that voice that grownups get when kids ask questions they're not supposed to ask. Well, Claire, I'm a grownup now, so get over it.

"Haven't heard from her or you or anybody since she ran off to your place."

Silence.

"I gotta go, say hi to Hannah for me." And I hang up the phone. Damn bitch. I'm so mad I'm trembling, looking for somebody to hit or something to break. I almost wish those guys would come back.

It takes me a good half hour and another glass of shine, the regular stuff, to calm down. By that time all I want to do is eat a bite of something and go to bed.

Chapter Twenty-Seven

I wake up the next day and make a cup of coffee, grab a handful of cereal out of the box, and go into the living room. Sitting on the couch, I think about the last few weeks.

I've been shot at and wounded by a friend of mine, somebody tried to break into my house, my Momma has evidently run off with some guy named Jake, I finally got to kiss a girl and she got up and ran out of the house, my friend, the one who shot me, is in the hospital and may or may not get out, and I can't remember anything else but I'm sure there's something I'm leaving out.

Frankie comes up and puts her head on the couch right next to me. I reach over and give her ears a scratch, and the phone rings.

It's Carrie.

"Boone, you better get down here," she says.

"What's going on?" I can't tell from her voice why I need to get down there.

"Just get here when you can. Sooner is better," she says, and hangs up the phone.

I pull on some clothes and give Frankie some food, jump in the truck, and head out. By the time I get there I've made up all kinds of stories about what's going on, none of them good. Carrie is in the lobby and gets up when she sees me come in.

"Come with me."

"What's going on, Carrie?"

We're not heading toward ICU. I remember it was to the right of the big front desk, and we're going straight ahead.

"Where are we going?"

She doesn't answer, just keeps walking, and then turns into a doorway. I follow her into what looks like a little church.

Jerry is there, and a woman, and other than that, the room is empty. It's very quiet in here. I look from one person to the other and my bad feelings get worse and worse.

"Let's sit down over here," the woman says.

"Y'all need to tell me what the hell's going on here," I say, trying hard not to shout.

Jerry starts to say something and Carrie shushes him. "Boone, we need to talk to this woman, and I wanted you to be here. Jerry doesn't agree, but Pop is family, and I know he thinks of you that way too. So here you are. Just come over here. Please."

I don't look at Jerry. I'd be fine with not ever seeing that asshole again, but I kind of like Carrie and this sounds like a big deal. We go to the front of the chapel and sit on the first couple of pews. It's been forever since I've been in church.

The last time I remember being in church was when I was nine or so and Hannah was just born. Momma still took us; Daddy never darkened the door of any church, used to say preachers were money-grubbing liars. I always could take it or leave it, never seemed like he was talking to me anyway. Talking about me, maybe, and maybe that's what got Daddy so mad about the whole church thing. Maybe he felt like the preacher was talking about him all the time, and sometimes it sure sounded like it.

We used to get home from church and Daddy would start in on Momma. "Well, what'd the liar talk about this time? How much of my money did you give that son of a bitch? Did you leave enough for us to eat on and put gas in the truck? I got to get to work, you know that, right?" He'd go on and on until Momma finally said something back to him and then he'd go after her. Sundays were bad at our house.

So I don't have a good feeling about the room I'm in, and I don't like Jerry being in there, and Carrie looks real worried, and this woman's got that look on her face like she's going to tell us something we don't want to hear, but she thinks we need to.

Jerry says, "Let's hear it. You got us all here now." He looks at me like I'm to blame for whatever news we're about to get. I want to get up and go over, whisper in his ear, remind him of what happened the last time he took me on, but the woman starts talking and he shuts up.

"Mr. Everett is a very sick man," she says quietly. Beside me, Carries stiffens and draws in her breath.

"What's wrong with him?" she asks, just as quiet.

"He's had a minor stroke — " and I don't hear anything after that. I manage to stay upright, but that's about all I can do. That's why he didn't make any sense when he tried to talk out there in the back yard. That's why he couldn't get up. I understand now, and it scares the hell out of me. I realize that I don't have anybody else, anybody at all. The woman is still talking, and I try to start listening to her again.

" — and of course he'll need round-the-clock care while we see what progress he can make."

Carrie looks at Jerry and they both look at me. Oh, no, I think, there's no way I can do that. I can't take care of an old man, feed him, dress him, wipe his ass, no way at all. They look at each other and then Carrie motions for me to follow her out into the hallway.

"Listen, Boone, we need a big favor from you," she says, and I get ready to say no before it can go any farther.

Then she says, "Pop is coming home with us, of course, and we'll keep him as long as it takes. I know it's a lot to ask to have you take care of the place for us, you know, keep it up and all. I hate to ask and Jerry, well, Jerry doesn't like you very much. He thinks this is a bad idea, but he doesn't have any other ideas, so as soon as the doctors say we can move him, we're getting him out of here."

She stops and looks at me like I'm supposed to say something. I just stare at her.

She gets my look all wrong and says, "Of course we'll pay you to watch the place. It won't be much, I'm afraid."

My brain finally catches up and I start to say that I wouldn't accept any money, that Gamaliel is like family to me too, but I don't say that. I say, "Well, there'll be electricity to pay for and stuff like that."

"Then you'll do it? Oh, Boone, that's great! I knew I, I mean we, could count on you. And we'll pay you, we'll insist on that."

I think about when I tried to pay Gamaliel for cashing in that ticket and he told me I was being insulting. I didn't understand that then, and I don't understand it now. I don't feel insulted at all.

"Whatever you think's right, Carrie," is what I say to her.

She nods. "It's settled, then."

She and I go back in, she gives Jerry a nod and he rolls his eyes, and I think about giving him a smile or a wink but decide not to.

"When can I see him?" I ask the woman, who is standing there with Jerry.

"Not for a day or so," she says.

I turn to Carrie. "Give me a call, would you, when I can see him? I don't remember where y'all live, and I want to see him before you move him out of here."

She nods. "Of course."

"I'm going to go now," I say to her and don't bother with Jerry. I just want to get out of this room and out of this hospital. I don't like hospitals.

When I get home I sit on the couch and try not to think the stuff I'm thinking.

Why didn't I make Gamaliel go to the doctor after those guys attacked the house?

What if something that happened then made this happen?

Is this all my fault? What if the old guy dies?

I get up and start walking around, trying to get a handle on this. I'm feeling really guilty.

After a few minutes I'm tired of it and say to myself, the old guy told you not to call anybody, You were just doing what he said. He's got a right to decide that shit for himself. Besides, what were you supposed to do, drag him to the truck and tie him in? You were shot, remember? And he's the one that shot you. Don't forget that. You probably saved his life, you're the one that found him on the ground, got him to the hospital, damn straight you saved him. Don't forget that either.

I wonder how much Carrie is going to pay me. That should be easy money, just looking in on the house every now and then. I'll need to go through it and make sure that there's nothing else valuable in there, just in case somebody breaks in while I'm not up there. Frankie comes over and looks at me. She's been watching me pace around and now that I'm still she comes up and sits in front of me. Just sits there, looking up at me, until I remember that she hasn't been fed and she's probably out of water.

When I head to the kitchen she's right behind me, and, sure enough, she's out of food and almost out of water. After I take care of her, I take her outside and let her run. She's getting bigger and bigger, close to four months old now and not a runt anymore, and I'm thinking I need to do some training, but I don't have the slightest idea how to do that.

Chapter Twenty-Eight

It's two weeks before I hear from Carrie; I mean I get phone calls, but they're real short and she doesn't say much, just "No change" or "A little better" and then she practically slams the phone down. I was mad the first time or two, but I figure she's really worried about her daddy and she's not doing it on purpose. This time she stays on the line, like she's got some news.

"Pop is almost ready to move, Boone," she says and pauses. "He can have visitors, but I need to let you know he's not doing so good."

I wait because I don't know what to say to that. I was going to yell at her for not calling, but this sounds bad.

There's a catch in her voice when she says, "He can't talk, Boone, his right side is affected too, he knows we're in the room, but there's not a lot of communicating going on. Just wanted you to know in advance."

"Thanks," I say.

The visit is awful. First, it's in a hospital, second, Jerry's there glaring at me the whole time, third, it's not the kind of place Gamaliel would want to spend even a minute.

But the worst is standing next to the bed watching him watch me. I can tell he's got stuff to say to me but he can't say it. Can't even ask for food or the bedpan or anything. It's awful. I stand there for a few minutes and then lean over so my mouth is right next to his ear.

"They want me to watch the house for you," I whisper to him. "I'll go up there every day and look around, okay?"

I step back and watch him. He looks at me and the side of his face that works kind of looks like a smile, but I figure I'm imagining that. So I just nod and get out of there as quick as I can.

Carrie follows me out. She hands me an envelope.

"There's two hundred dollars in there," she says, a little unsteady. "Let me know what the bills are and we'll kind of figure it out as we go."

I can tell she's about to cry, so I try to think of something to say to make it better. I can't think of anything.

"You let me know how he's doing, okay?" I finally say, and realize that I'm about to cry too. There's no way she's going to see that, so I turn to leave. She grabs my arm.

"Boone? You know he's probably not coming back to that house, don't you?"

I shake my head. "We don't know that, Carrie."

She looks at me like I've lost my mind. "Did you see him in there? Did you? There is no way he could stay in that place, no way." Her voice is rising and I'm thinking she's going to start shouting any second. The door opens and Jerry steps out. He looks at Carrie and then at me.

"What'd you say to her, you little shit? You've got her all upset on top of what's happened to her daddy. What's wrong with you?"

I take a step toward him and he backs up. He can tell by the look in my eye that I don't care if we're in a hallway with people all around us, I'll jump him. I don't mind a bit.

He turns back to Carrie, "Come on, darling, let's go back in. You," he glances at me, "don't you have someplace to be besides here?"

Other people are looking at me as they pass and I realize that my fists are tight and my face is red. Carrie looks up at me, her face streaked with tears.

"You better go, Boone. We'll let you know how things go with Pop."

She and Jerry go back inside and I'm left standing there like a fool. After a minute I shake out my hands and go back out to the truck.

What I want is somebody besides Frankie to talk to. I've been here since I got back, all morning and part of the afternoon sitting on the couch thinking about Gamaliel lying there in that bed, or doing the same thing at Carrie's house, and it's making me crazy. I'm thinking I should've let the old man die there in his own yard, and I know that's dangerous thinking but I can't help it and I know I need somebody to talk to about something else, anything else, and there's nobody.

Frankie is lying there in front of the TV and every once in a while she'll look up at me and then put her head back down. I wish she could talk back, I try to tell her stuff and she listens, I know she's listening, but it's just not the same.

The phone rings and I'm off the couch and running for it, I get it by the second ring.

"Hello?"

"Hey, Boone, it's me."

Nancy sounds like nothing special is going on, and I guess in her world nothing is.

"How's it going?"

"I was going to ask you that. Okay if I come over later on?"

"Sure, I may not be much good company."

245

"What's wrong, Boone?" she sounds really concerned, and I like that, hearing that.

"My neighbor's in the hospital."

"I'm so sorry. What's wrong?"

"I found him lying in his back yard a couple of weeks ago. He went into the hospital, and then a few days later Carrie, that's his daughter, she called me. The docs say he had a stroke. I was there today, he doesn't look good."

"I'll be right over."

I start to tell her not to worry, that I'm okay, but she's already hung up the phone.

I go back into the living room and sit down, and then get right back up. She's about fifteen minutes by car from here, so she'll be here before long. The place is a wreck, but I'm not about to try to fix that. What I need right now is a little shine, I decide.

There's a new two liter in the fridge, so I finish off the old one and top the glass off, take a sip, and go outside to wait for Nancy. It's chilly, but I like this time of year, before the cold really settles in. The sun is starting to get that winter look, kind of pale and far off, and the wind is moving the branches against each other. Fits my mood. I take another drink and call Frankie over. I had seen her go around the house right after I let her out.

She doesn't come, and I call her again. Then I hear a noise from around back. When I turn the corner Frankie's looking away from the house, toward the woods, and I think I see movement back there.

I'm back in a second with the shotgun, which I remember to load this time, and I head toward the woods, Frankie right beside me. There's definitely somebody up there, and I shout, "Y'all get off my land! Now!"

It sounds like laughing coming from up the hill towards the fence line, and I put the stock on my shoulder and point to the sky. When I pull the trigger I think, damn, I'd forgotten about the kick this thing has.

It sure works, though, because I can hear the leaves and branches and catch glimpses of a couple of people up there, running for their lives. I reach down to scratch behind Frankie's ear.

"Good girl, Frankie, good girl."

"Boone, are you all right? Where are you, Boone?"

Nancy's voice comes from around front, frantic, and I trot back to the edge of the house. She's standing behind the car door, and I can see from where I am how scared she is.

I shout to her that I'm all right, and go inside to put the gun back in the closet. Frankie goes up to Nancy to investigate. By the time I get to her, she's back against the back door of the car and Frankie's standing in front of her. Well, I think, she's seen the surprise.

Frankie steps toward her and she puts out a hand, gingerly, and Frankie sniffs at it and her tail wags a little. Then she sits right in front of Nancy and I swear she cocks her head to the side and grins at her.

Nancy laughs out loud.

"Where did you find her, Boone? She's great!" Then she turns serious. "Was that you shooting? What were you shooting at?"

"Couple of houses been broken into up here," I say. "There were two guys in the woods behind the house. I shot up into the air and they took off. Frankie saw them first," and I reach down to scratch behind her ear.

"Have they stolen anything from you?"

I shake my head. "Nah, not much here to steal, I just don't want them to think they can waltz in here whenever they want. They tried to break into Gamaliel's house the other day," and as soon as I say that I turn and head back into the house.

When I come out with the shotgun Nancy's eyes widen.

"What are you getting ready to do, Boone?"

I point up the hill. "His house is right up there, and I just scared them off of my property. Going up to take a look. You wait here, house is open. I'll be right back. They probably just kept going when I scared them, but he's in the hospital, and I'm supposed to look after his place. I'll be right back," I repeat, and head for the truck.

"I'm going to call the police," she says, and heads for the kitchen door.

"Don't," I say, and she turns around.

"Why not?"

"Because I didn't get broken into, the people on my property are gone, and I don't even know if anything's wrong up at his house. You know how far they have to drive to get here. What do you think they'd say if they made the trip for nothing? I gotta go, don't do anything. If they're already up there I'll come back and we'll call."

"Promise?"

I make an X on my chest. "Cross my heart."

Nancy smiles a little. "You be careful, Boone."

I'm already in the truck and backing up. I barely miss her door; she left it open when she got out of the car, but I miss it and get the truck headed up the hill.

Chapter Twenty-Nine

They're up there all right, but just on their way to the back door, and when I pull the truck into the tracks that run beside the house and they see me getting out with the shotgun in my hand they take off again. I take a quick look around; no doors or windows busted out, and I wait a few minutes and decide to go on back down to the house.

Nancy is still waiting for me and runs up to the truck.

"Well?"

I nod at her and open the door; she steps back enough to let me out and starts to grab me until she sees the shotgun.

"Can you go put that thing up, please? It scares me."

"Sure," I say and head toward the house, Nancy and Frankie right behind me. I go straight to the closet and lean the gun against the side wall, close the door, and turn around. "Okay?"

I barely get the word out before she's got such a hold on me I can hardly draw breath. I'm thinking I need to chase off burglars more often, maybe every time she's here. I put my arms around her and we stand there for a second, and I'm thinking this is the best I've felt in years, maybe ever. I can feel myself starting to get hard and I guess she feels it too, because she breaks loose and steps back a little, looking everywhere except in my face.

"Want to go sit down?" I finally say, because we're both pretty uncomfortable.

Nancy nods and we head back down the hallway. When we pass Momma and Daddy's room she glances in and then away and I wish I had kept the door closed. It's still just like it was, a godawful mess, broken mirror and all. I don't want to have to explain that to her.

We get back to the living room and she says, "You sure you're okay, Boone? I was scared for you. That sure was a brave thing, going up there all by yourself." She's looking at me like nobody's ever done before.

I'm really afraid I'll say something stupid, so I don't say anything at all. I just stand there.

After what seems like a long time, she says, "I think I'd like something to drink. Got anything in the fridge, Boone?"

I'm about to offer her a little shine and then think that's about the stupidest thing I could do right now. I don't really know her at all, and what if she went home and spread that all over town? No telling what kind of trouble I'd be in. So I say, "Thunderstorm Soda is all, and there's water."

"Water'd be good," she says, and sounds a little disappointed. I go get her a glass and drop a couple of ice cubes in it. I get my drink and put ice in it too and carry them both back.

"Here you go," I say and hand it to her.

She says thanks and we sit down on the couch, a little distance between us. I think about the last time we were on this couch.

She takes a sip of water. "Tell me about your friend," she says.

I take a drink and set the glass down. Where to start? How much do I tell her? Not everything, that's for sure.

"I don't know how exactly to tell you about Gamaliel," I said.

"What is his name?"

"Gamaliel."

"That's an odd name."

I look at Nancy, sitting there on the couch, telling me my only friend has a funny name, and I'm mad at her, all of a sudden. She catches me looking at her and turns a little red.

"I don't mean odd in a bad way, Boone, I kind of like the name. It's strong, you know? You just don't hear that name very much, or even at all. I don't know anybody else with that name. How did you get to know him?"

She's trying really hard to make up for what she did, I can tell, and that helps some.

"He lives up the hill from me, and I needed to borrow something once a while back, and I guess it started from that."

She nods and doesn't say anything. I guess she wants me to keep going.

"He's a great guy, I like spending time up there. Not too much going on down here these days," I say and then think that I'm an idiot.

"I mean except for right now."

She smiles a little. I sit back and think for a minute.

"One of the first times I saw him, he was in this really dark room, like an old person's living room, you know, lots of pictures and heavy furniture and no light?" She nods. "Anyway, he was sitting in there with a fiddle on the floor in front of him and he was singing that old just a closer walk hymn, and crying. He wouldn't tell me what he was so sad about, he ran me out, told me to go on home."

"That's so sad, Boone. Do you think somebody died or something like that?"

I shrug. "I guess so." I'm not ready to talk to her about that. "Anyway, I went back a couple of days later and he was better and I started going up there a lot."

"I bet he likes that." She pauses. "Boone, what happened to the rest of your family? Hannah's not in school either, and nobody's seen your parents in the longest time."

I don't want to talk about this.

"I thought you said you wanted to hear about Gamaliel," I say, and I can hear the scared kid in my voice.

Nancy hears anger, I guess, because her face tightens and she starts to get up. I want to keep her here but I don't know what to say, so I don't say anything, I just reach out my hand.

She looks at it and then up at me. "Boone, I don't know what all's going on with you. It's like you're mad all the time. Sometimes you scare me. Maybe I should get out of here."

"No," I say, and let my hand drop down on the couch. I swallow hard and say, "Can you stay and talk to me just a minute?"

She just stands there for a second, and then it's like she remembers why she came running over here in the first place.

"Okay," she says, "let's talk about Gamaliel. So you started going up there? What do you do? I mean, it sounds like he likes having you there. You just talk and stuff?"

I try to think about what Gamaliel and I talk about besides how to make shine and how it tastes, and it takes me a minute. "We talk about his family some, he's lived up there for a long time, knows a lot about the town and all the people. He and the Thompson clan get along just fine. I don't think those guys trying to rob us were Thompsons. Mrs. Thompson would kick their ass good if it was them and she found out. So I don't know who they were, and I don't know whether or not to tell Gamaliel about it when I go see him next."

"Don't," Nancy says firmly. "He needs to get better. Besides, you took care of it, right?"

I look at her and she's looking at me like she thinks I did something really amazing, and I get embarrassed and drop my head. I'm still looking down when I feel her hands on my head, sliding down to my shoulders. Then the couch creaks a little and I feel her right beside me. She's rubbing my arms and then she takes my head in her hands and raises it and I look at her in the eyes and they're bright and a little teary, and the look in her eyes is like an animal, like she's completely focused on right now. Her cheeks are redder than I remember.

"What if you'd had to fight them, Boone?" She's whispering now. "Are you strong enough for that?"

255

I'm strong, I think, damn right I'm strong. I grab her shoulders and turn her and now her back's against the couch and I'm looking down into that face and her eyes are locked on mine. She's breathing faster now, and I realize I am too. My heart feels like it's about to jump right out of my chest. I lean toward her, toward those red lips, and she pulls me the last half inch and we're kissing like I dreamed we would, I can feel her tongue with mine and her hands are on my back pulling me hard toward her. I'm holding myself with my hands against the couch and I shift my weight to my left. My right hand is on her shoulder now and I move down to her breast and there's barely room between us for me to move my hand, but I drop it down and slide it under her shirt and back up to her bra and all the time we're still kissing and my head is spinning, it's like being drunk. Hell, it's better than being drunk.

Then she's pushing me away from her, and I'm wondering, is she testing me, does she want to know how strong I am? I start to lean in harder and her hand is on my wrist and she jerks my hand out from under her shirt and ducks and slides out underneath me and stands up next to the couch.

I'm strong enough, I think to myself, and I push myself off the couch and now we're standing next to each other, almost touching, and I reach out to take her arm and pull her to me.

Nancy takes a step back and now I'm really confused. Now it's like she doesn't want me even close to her. I look at her and her eyes are still wild but there's something else there.

She and I are looking at each other across the open space, and the wildness starts to fade and all that's left is fear. She's afraid of me.

"Boone I know if I stay here any longer I — I — " she stops, takes a breath, and continues, "I really want to stay but I'd better not. Do you understand, Boone? Please don't be mad at me."

Hell, no, I don't understand.

"You didn't like what we were doing?"

She shakes her head hard, left and right. "I liked it a lot, that's the problem."

"It doesn't have to be any kind of problem," I say and take a step toward her. She backs up and says, "I can't, Boone, I can't. You know I can't."

She's in the kitchen before I can even move and I'm close but not close enough to grab her. I go after her, thinking, if I can just get a hand on her I'll keep her here, I'm strong enough.

Then she's in her car, the door closed, and she's crying, leaning her head against the steering wheel. I tap on the window and nothing happens.

"I'm sorry, I'm sorry, just get out of the car. We can just talk, Nancy, come on back in. Or we could sit out here if you want to."

She's shaking her head no, no, no, and I don't tap on the door anymore. I hit the windshield hard and she jumps, then puts the key in the ignition and starts the car. She's backing out fast and I'm chasing the car like a damn dog, pounding on the hood.

She gets the car into the road, shifts into drive, and takes off like a rabbit, and just like that she's gone.

Chapter Thirty

I'm standing in the front yard looking like a damn fool when I see a car come over the hill. I'm not sure who it is so I get back in the house as quick as I can. There's some soda left and I make an S&S, mostly shine, and stand there in the kitchen and drink it all down fast.

What the hell is wrong with her? She was right in there with me, she didn't mind, I think she liked it. I know I did. So what happened? Then I remember that one time a while back when I told her I had some shine and she asked if she could taste it, and I'm kicking myself because she was here and I didn't offer and maybe that would have made things different and I realize I don't have any idea what I'm talking about.

I will never understand women, I say to myself, and then Frankie comes into the kitchen. She sits in front of me and looks up, then looks at the door.

"You want to go out, girl?"

She trots over to the door and stands there, tail wagging, ready.

I laugh and go over to the door. A little unsteady on my feet. I drank that kind of fast, I realize. I open the door to let her out and Nancy is standing there. Guess it was her car coming over the hill.

"Thought you were gone."

She's looking everywhere but at me. "Aren't you going to ask me why I came back?"

I shrug. I'm still pretty unsteady, don't know whether I should try to say something or not.

Wasn't even sure that last thing I said came out right.

She looks up at me and says, "Would you take me up to Gamaliel's house?"

My first thought is why the hell does she want to go up there? My second thought is no, that's my place, mine and Gamaliel's. Nobody else's. I'm mad and confused and kind of drunk and Frankie needs to go outside, so I open the door and she slips out between me and Nancy.

Finally I say, "Not today, Nancy. Those guys, whoever they are, might come back. I was thinking I should go up there, take a look around."

"Well, I want to go along."

I shake my head. "Don't want anything to happen to you."

She looks up at me. "Ten minutes ago you were really mad at me, and now you're worried?"

I don't know what I'm feeling about this whole thing. What I want is to go back to the couch, but I know that's not happening.

"I said I was sorry about that," I say.

"No, you said that before you started banging on my car. On my daddy's car."

"So why do you want to go up there anyway?" I don't want to think about me and the car. Too much like something Daddy would do.

"I want to see where you chased those guys off from." Her face is getting red, but she keeps going. "I didn't want to run out on you, Boone, honest, but I was afraid of what we might do. I still think it was brave, what you did, and I guess I wanted to see that."

So she did like it. I want to grab her, drag her back inside, but I can't make myself do that. Daddy again. I can't turn out that way, I can't. I won't. I know what I'll do if she stays around though.

"I'll take you some other time, I promise. If you're afraid of what we were about to do in there you should go on home. It's better, doing that, going home I mean, you know?"

She can see it in my face, I think, because she nods slowly and says, "I think you're right. I'll call you, okay?"

She turns around to go back to her car and I hear her say, "I'll call you. I will."

She leaves, slower this time, and I go back inside. Then I turn around and go out, call Frankie, and get in the truck to go check on Gamaliel's house.

The next day the phone rings and it's Nancy.

"Boone, did you hear?"

"Hear what?"

"Those guys, those guys you ran off. They caught them."

Until this minute I did not know how worried I was. I say, trying to sound calm, "You sure it was the same guys?"

"I think so, Boone. Two guys, on a four-wheeler, they were trying to break into somebody's house on the other side of town. I don't know the guy, but he had a couple of dogs and turned them loose and they tore those boys up pretty bad. He had to haul the dogs off one at a time, but they're still alive and in the hospital, at least that's what I hear. You have to go to the police, Boone, maybe you can identify them. I'll bet it's the same guys."

"I can't do that, Nancy. You can't tell anybody they were up here."

There's a silence that goes on for a while. Then she says, "I don't understand. Don't you want them to pay for what they tried to do?"

"Seems like they're already paying. Anyway, I just want to stay out of the whole thing. Sounds like they won't be bothering me again, and that's what I want. Don't tell anybody about them being up here, Nancy. Promise that."

She hesitates and then says, "Okay, Boone, I won't say anything. But I think you're wrong about this. I do."

I wonder if I can trust her. The last thing I want is a bunch of police snooping around up here. They might find the still. Hell, they might find the shine I've got stashed in the barn. They might find the money I've got up in the pool under those rocks. No way I want anybody around here. Now I wish she hadn't been up here when I ran those guys off. I think about telling her that if she tells I'll tell her daddy she let me do a lot more than put my hand up her shirt. That might actually work, I realize.

But I'd never get to do it again. I know that for sure, so I decide not to tell her that. Then I remember I'm still on the phone with her and hope like hell I didn't say any of that out loud. Try as hard as I can, I can't remember the last thing she said. So now I don't know what to say. I need to say something, though.

"So, those guys, they're in the hospital? Pretty torn up, were they?"

She's not happy with me, I can tell that by the way she answers me. "Yeah, I guess. Listen, I got homework, you know? Maybe I'd better go."

"You coming up sometime soon? I mean, since they aren't around any more, I can show you Gamaliel's place and not have to worry."

"I don't know, Boone, maybe." She doesn't sound like she's going to come back.

"You know I was just worried about you, You know that, right?"

She doesn't answer right away. "Yeah, I know."

I've run out of stuff to say.

"Listen," I say, "I need to feed Frankie and check on stuff. Come back up, okay? Frankie says she misses you already."

Nancy laughs and I think, good girl, Frankie.

"Okay, I'll see you in a day or two."

"Call first so you'll know I'm here and not back at the pool or up at Gamaliel's."

"What pool? You said something once, but never told me about it."

"Oh, just a place where the creek widens out and slows down. It's kind of deep in the middle. I like it up there, especially in the summer. It's good all the time, though."

"Well, when were you going to show me this pool? Can you swim in it?"

I laugh, and so does she. "Not now, unless you like it really cold. I've never taken a swim in it, just go up there and sit. It's quiet except for the water sounds and, you know, birds and stuff like that."

"Will you show it to me?"

She's not mad anymore, I can tell that. Maybe she'll keep her mouth shut about those guys coming over here.

"Sure, next time you come up wear some shoes you can wear into the woods and be sure and come while it's still light."

"You afraid of the dark, Boone?"

For just a second I'm mad and then I realize she's teasing me.

"No, I like it up there in the dark. It's great, like it's someplace far away from here."

"See, now you have to show it to me. First time in the daylight, like you said, but it sounds really nice in the dark."

Now I don't know what to say again. I don't know how to do this kind of stuff, I'd never ask Daddy, Momma's gone, and Gamaliel might be gone pretty soon. What the hell do I say?

"Okay."

Now that was stupid.

"I mean, sure, I'll take you up there. Nobody knows it's there, really, it's on the back part of the farm, and it's in the woods, so we don't grow anything up there."

Now she's quiet. Then she says, "Sounds nice. I'll be sure and call, make sure you don't have another girl there before I come over."

Is she teasing me again? I think she is.

"You don't need to worry about that, Nancy," I say real quick. I want to get done with this before I say something really stupid.

"Well, I got studying, so I'll see you later."

"Okay," I say, and she hangs up.

I don't hear from her or Carrie or anybody for three or four days. I don't think much about what day it is, not anymore. The school hasn't called, and hasn't sent any letters. I guess the whole Mr. Timmons thing is all they're thinking about now, and that's fine by me. I don't plan to go back unless I'm made to.

The next time the phone rings it's Carrie.

"Boone, I just wanted you to know how Pop is doing. He's okay, considering everything. He's talking, but he has trouble with some of his words, you know? But he's coming along, they say."

"That's good," I say. "I'd like to come see him if that's all right. I don't think Jerry wants me anywhere near y'all."

"He's gone back up to the house to get a room ready for Pop," she says. "They say we can move him in a week or so, that he'll be okay at home with somebody to look after him."

"That's good, right?"

She sounds really tired. "I guess so, but he's still not in very good shape, Boone. Better than the last time you saw him, so if you want to come down and see him I think he'd like that."

"I will, Carrie, I will. How about tomorrow morning?"

She says that'd be good and hangs up quick. I think she's worn out.

Chapter Thirty-One

Frankie and I take a turn around the property. It's warm for winter, just right for running the dog. We head up past the field where Daddy is and I can't even tell where the grave is and I'm the one who dug it. I've just about stopped worrying about that. The fall went on so long that the kudzu and everything else grew up and there's not even a mound anymore.

The path to the pool is easier to see in this season, so Frankie and I are there in no time. This is my best place, no question. I come up slow, thinking about Nancy walking in front of me.

Frankie doesn't share my reluctance to swim; she's in the pool immediately, even though the water's gotta be damn cold. It's cool even in the August heat, and we're way past August. She loves it, splashing across to the other side of the pool and clambering out, shaking herself dry and then looking over at me.

"Let's check the still, girl," I say, and she meets me at the head of the pool and jumps across the stream and we head off into the woods. Why I didn't get a dog a long time ago is beyond me, I think to myself.

The still is right where and how we left it and I'm sad all of a sudden, thinking about how I was going to get Gamaliel to show me how to make shine, all the steps, not just what we did. I can remember what we did together, but I need that first little bit. I'm not worried, I've got a lot of shine, especially if I don't have to share. That thought makes me even sadder and I think I need to get down to the hospital and see the old man.

When I get back to the house the sun's close to setting; long shadows and grey and brown everywhere around me. Frankie and I go into the house and I find a can of soup, open it up, and sit in the kitchen eating soup and crackers. Frankie watches me for a while and then goes into the living room. I follow her in and fall back on the couch. I know it's because I was sad already, but now I'm thinking about my brother Frankie and how we lost him. And how that might have been the thing that finished Daddy off.

I really can't remember what Daddy was like before Frankie died, so I might be wrong about that part. It feels like things just bottomed out after

Frankie and never came back up. I know it just about did Momma in; Hannah was kind of young, so she probably bounced back farther than any of the rest of us. It wasn't long before she stopped asking about Frankie, mainly because it made Momma cry and Daddy mad as hell. Then he'd take it out on everybody else, mostly me, or at least it seemed like it was mostly me.

I remember Frankie could make Momma and Daddy laugh, something I never could do. We'd be sitting around the table and Frankie would tell a story from school and all the time he'd be making those silly faces to go with the story and pretty soon either Momma or Daddy would be laughing and wiping their eyes and for a minute we'd forget how mean Daddy was most of the time and how Momma had to serve the same beans and cornbread four or five times a week because there wasn't any money. I guess sometimes I really hated him because he could do that and I couldn't. Most of the time, though, I didn't hate Frankie. He was my best and maybe my only friend.

Then we were playing around in the barn that day and he was showing off, like he did sometimes. He climbed up on one of the cross pieces and was going to do a back flip and his foot slipped when he was taking off and he landed wrong. He got right back up and brushed off all the hay and dirt and went right on. When we got back to the house Momma asked him how he got cut. Neither one of us had even noticed it, because it was on the back of his arm, up high close to the shoulder. Momma washed it off and we didn't think any more about it.

Two or three days later we were just fooling around and I smacked him on the arm, didn't even remember that he'd ben cut, and he yelled and grabbed it and I could tell it hurt. Turned out it had got all red and swollen and he just thought it'd go away by itself. When Momma saw how angry red it was she scrubbed it so hard it made Frankie cry and took a needle and held it in a flame and then poked at it. That really set him off, but he held still while she squeezed a whole lot of pus out of it. She put a bandage on it and kept looking at it two or three times a day after that. She wanted to take him to the doctor but Daddy said we couldn't afford to, those damn doctors were all thieves, tell you something's wrong just to sell you another pill. I can still hear him saying that, and Momma getting more scared every day.

When Frankie couldn't get out of bed and was burning up with fever, Daddy finally gave in and we went to the doctor. As soon as he saw Frankie's arm he told us go straight to the hospital and he'd call ahead and get us a room.

271

I never will forget that fight between Momma and Daddy. I'd never seen her stand up to him like that, before or since, and he was fighting just as hard, saying we couldn't afford a hospital bill, that she needed to go back in there and get a pill or something and Frankie just sitting in the back seat kind of slumped down.

They fought about that all that day and the next and finally Momma won and we went to the hospital. By that time it was too late. The doctors explained it, or tried to, and Daddy wouldn't listen, he was crazy mad, blamed the doctors and the hospital and Momma and me and everybody but Hannah. And himself, but now that I look back I think maybe he blamed himself most of all and that's why he turned so dark and angry and pretty much never smiled again, much less laughed. He'd never admit that though, that he might have had some fault. I know he acted like he hated pretty much everything and everybody after that, and it never let up. Momma just went way inside herself and Daddy, well, I was glad in a way when he finally did himself with that shotgun.

When I saw him there on the barn floor, I think I saw a way to put it all away from me for good. I didn't think about it, I just wanted him gone, out of sight, in the ground. I think if Momma had known about it, him being dead, I mean, she would have come back, but I don't think she could have been in this house, with all the sadness all around, everywhere you look. I don't know. I think she would have left again, or maybe not even come back at all. I know I couldn't have stayed, they wouldn't have let me, being underage and all.

I don't like thinking about this, not at all. I go get a glass and fill it half with shine and start to mix it with something and I remember Gamaliel always drank his straight. So I take it back to the couch, sit down, and turn on the TV to get something in my head to run off the memories. And I remember to sip, not swig.

The next day it's almost noon before I get up and I have to move slow or I'll start throwing up. I get a little cereal in my stomach and that helps, and I take Frankie out and let her run for a while and then I go back in and lie down. In about a minute I'm asleep and don't wake up until the phone rings.

It's Carrie.

"You still planning to come by, Boone?"

I shake my head and look at the clock in the kitchen. Three in the afternoon.

"Sorry, Carrie, had a hard time sleeping last night and I've been kind of out of it this morning. Still okay if I come by, or should I wait?"

"No, come on. I actually told him you'd be by this morning, since that's what you said," and I can hear

273

the disapproval in her voice. For a second I'm mad, like who the hell is she to get on my case, and then it passes and I say, "Tell Gamaliel I'll be there in half an hour."

"I think I'll just wait until you get here," she says.

"Okay, see you soon," I say and hang up.

Frankie's looking at me when I turn around. She goes over to the door and sits down, looking at it and then at me.

"I don't have time for this, girl," I say, and just then the phone rings again.

"Hello?"

"Boone, it's Carrie. Pop just had to be taken up to surgery, something went wrong, I don't know, you probably can't see him, just wanted you to not waste a trip." She's right on the edge of crying, I can tell, and I don't know what to do about that.

"Listen, Carrie, I'm coming down there to sit with you. Jerry's gone, right?"

"He's back home, getting Pop's room ready."

"Then I'm coming down to sit with you. I want to be there when he gets out of surgery."

"You know you don't have to do that," she says, but I can tell she wants me to come. She's got that fake polite tone in her voice, like that's what she's supposed to say, but it's not what she wants to happen.

"See you in a little bit, just have to let the dog run for a minute," I say, and hang up.

Chapter Thirty-Two

When I get there she's in the waiting room pacing back and forth, and she runs up to me as soon as she sees me and throws her arms around me. I'm glad I came and scared to death for Gamaliel all at the same time.

She backs off and wipes her eyes.

"It was a blood clot in his leg," she says.

I guess I must look as stupid as I feel, because she goes on.

"Sometimes that happens after a stroke, I guess, and they had to go in and remove it. If they hadn't, it might have killed the muscle in that leg or it might have moved into his lung and that would have been really bad."

I nod because I can't think of anything to say.

"He's still in there but I think surely it's time for them to be finished," she says nervously. "Don't you think so, Boone?"

I nod again. Feeling really helpless, plus I don't like hospitals, plus I'm worried about Gamaliel.

It seems like hours before the docs come out but when I look at the clock I've only been here 45 minutes or so. Gamaliel came through it okay, he's in recovery, should be all right, they say. Carrie is crying and smiling at the same time, and I'm close to crying myself.

"You know this means we can't discharge him for a while," they're saying to Carrie when I start listening again.

She says, "I kind of assumed that. How long do you think it will be?"

The surgeon thinks for a minute and then says, "I didn't have to make a very large incision, but he is getting on in years. Let's decide that tomorrow or the next day. He'll need care for quite a while after he's discharged, you know."

"I know," she says, and her voice is tired, even though it's early in the evening.

She goes back over to one of the couches and plops down.

Carrie looks back at me and I guess she can tell I'm stuck. I know I'm supposed to stay and keep her company and wait for news on Gamaliel, but I really hate hospitals.

"Boone, why don't you go on home?" she says.

"I should stay," I reply, but I don't go over to her or sit down or anything.

She smiles a little. "You really hate being here, I can see that. Go check on Gamaliel's house for me. I'll call you at your house later and tell you how he is doing."

"You sure?"

That's what I'm supposed to say, I know that, but I don't want her to withdraw the offer.

She nods. "Get out of here; I need to call Jerry and let him know he's got a little more time to work on Pop's room."

"Okay, Carrie. You call me, okay?"

"I will," she says.

Gamaliel's house is dark when I get there; I pull in thinking maybe I should leave a light burning so people will think he's still there. The road doesn't get a lot of traffic and almost no strangers, so it's probably not necessary, but I'm thinking I'll do it anyway.

I go in the back door and turn on some lights. It feels strange and wrong, somehow, to be here without him, but I take my time going through the house. No reason I can think of to go into his bedroom, so I leave that alone. I stand in the front room for a while, thinking about the first time I saw him in there, crying for his lost son.

We never talked about that, him losing his kid. At first I was afraid to bring it up and then we just sort of didn't talk about it, like we didn't talk about Frankie and what happened to him. The old man and I know each other pretty well now, done some stuff together, hell, he shot me and then fixed me up, and it still doesn't feel right, asking him about his son. I realize I don't even know the kid's name.

Standing there in that dark room with all those family pictures around, I promise myself that when he gets back up here I'm going to do two things.

I'm going to talk to him about Frankie. I haven't done that, me and Momma and Daddy never brought it up, and I think Daddy would have beat us if any of us had said anything. Looking back, I bet the guilt was killing him a little every day. He never came back to my room, and I bet that's because Momma kept Frankie's side just like it was. Like one of those shrines I heard about in school before I stopped paying attention. I'm thinking I'll just bring it up sometime, after a couple of glasses, and tell him the story if he's interested in hearing it. One thing about Gamaliel, if he's not interested, he'll let you know right off. I think I can get through it, and it might get him started talking about his kid. I really don't know much about his family at all, now that I think about it. I know about Carrie, but not very much, and I don't know anything about his wife or if he had more than one. We need to talk about more than shine, I say to myself, when he gets back up here. But that brings up the other thing I'm going to do when Gamaliel gets back home.

I'm going to get him to teach me how to make shine. Just the first part; I know how to do the last, the boiling and filtering and all that, but I don't know about the first part. He needs to tell me about that.

Because he might not be going back up to the still. He might not be coming back here at all, and I don't like thinking about that. I really like the old guy. I don't have anybody else around here to talk to.

As I'm leaving, I decide to go out into the tool shed and check that out. It's been a while since I did that, and it's always possible that those two thieves cleaned out the shed before they decided to hit the house. I go up to the shed and pull open the door.

I breathe a sigh of relief when I see the inside of the shed. It doesn't look like anybody's been here since I was here filtering that batch of shine with Gamaliel. I've never spent any time in the shed, so I decide to have a close look around.

Just as quick I change my mind; Carrie is going to call when she knows something about Gamaliel, and I want to be there to get the update. Besides, I've seen enough to be able to tell her everything's all right here, and, since Nancy told me about those two guys getting caught, I'm really not too worried about leaving his place for the night. I can give her the news about his place and maybe she'll have some good news about him. I realize that I care a lot about him. He's been a lot nicer to me than he had to be.

Maybe, I think as I get back in the truck and head down to my house, maybe he's glad to have some company too. I try to remember anybody going up to see him and, except for the guy with the bad news about his son and his daughter and her asshole husband, I can't think of anybody at all.

Nothing that night from Carrie, but she calls the next morning and says he's doing as well as could be expected. He's started to give the nurses a hard time, which Carrie says is good. She tells me he never has been a good patient, always wanting to get out of bed and go back home. I tell her I know just how he feels.

"He asked about you this morning, Boone," she says. "You should come by and see him."

This time I make it, thinking all the time that I'm going to need to figure out some way to get a license one of these days. I'm okay as long as I don't go much of anywhere, but I'd still like to have one.

Gamaliel is flat on his back, but he's got his bed cranked up a little and he gives me a wink when he sees me at the door. I wave and say hi to Carrie. She's sitting in a chair next to the window.

She looks a little better than she did yesterday, but not much. Running on no sleep, I guess, and I know exactly how that feels. When Frankie — I stop, force myself to think about Gamaliel instead of my dead brother, and then go the rest of the way in.

They're both looking at me strangely.

"What was that?" said Carrie.

"What was what?"

"That look on your face," she says. "You were lost somewhere else for a second. Are you okay?"

"Fine," I say and I know nobody in the room believes that.

"How are you, old man?" I ask, to try to get things moving on to something else.

He shakes a fist at me, barely lifting his hand off the bed. "Don't call me old . . . boy, I'll . . . . kick your a-a-a-ass for you."

Carrie laughs, probably, I think, the first one in a while. She nods at me.

"He's been waiting for someone to give him a hard time, Boone. I'm real glad you could make it in to see him."

I take a deep breath. Maybe we can talk about something besides me now. My idea of talking to Gamaliel about Frankie doesn't seem so good at the moment, even though when I was thinking about it yesterday, I had an image of me and him sitting in the sunroom passing a jar back and forth and just talking. It'll be quite a while before that happens, I say to myself. His speech is kind of slurry, like he's thinking a little faster than he can make the words.

"Listen, Carrie," I say, "Why don't you go get a cup of coffee or a sandwich or something? I'll keep an eye on Gamaliel for you. If he tries to leave, I'll stand in the door."

She gets up, stretches, and goes over to the bed.

"I'll be back in a few minutes, Pop," she says, and gives him a peck on the cheek.

On her way out the door, she puts her hand on my arm. "Thanks, Boone."

Chapter Thirty-Three

After she leaves, Gamaliel motions me over to the bed.

"How's . . . house?"

"It's good," I say. "I was just up there last night."

"Heard any more from those j-j-j-jack-offs that tried . . . rob me?"

I tell him what Nancy told me, and he nods his head.

"Serves them right." He looks blank for a second and then focuses on my face. "I'm real sorry I s-sh-sh-sh-shot you, Boone, I didn't mean to."

"It's all right," I say. "I heal quick, and now we don't have to worry about them any more."

"Sure-sure-sure it was them?"

"Well, I never saw them when they came after us, but the description fits. I'll keep my eyes open, but I think they're done for."

"Good. Now listen, Boone . . .there's something I need . . . tell you. In the sh-shed — "

Just then a nurse comes in and he scowls at her.

"Can't you see I'm . . . busy?" He waves a hand at her. It doesn't move much. "Get on out of here and c-c-c-come back tomorrow, or . . . next day."

She is about my height, younger than Momma, and pretty heavy. I don't like her.

She looks at me. "Are you family?"

"Hell, yes, family," Gamaliel says, trying to sit up.

"Now, Mr. Everett, you know you need to stay still so you can heal," she says, moving to the side of the bed and putting a hand on his chest.

He tries to smack her hand away, but he's pretty weak, plus his arm doesn't work like it did before. I step up to the other side of the bed.

"Why don't you let him be?"

She looks at me like I just crawled out from under her front porch.

"Mr. Everett needs his rest, Mr.?"

I don't answer her. I look over at Gamaliel and say, "Does she do this a lot, Gamaliel?"

Before he can answer, she says, "If you don't leave right now, young man, I'll have to call security."

"Why don't you just go ahead and call them," I say and then Gamaliel puts his hand on mine.

"Don't get yourself in trouble, Boone. Let her poke at me; I won't have to-to-to put up with her much longer."

I look right at him. "You sure? I'll stick around if you need me to."

"I know that . . . boy, I know. You get on out of here, go go go find Carrie and tell her you had to leave. Make sure the shed's all right. Look good, okay?"

He winks at me and says, "If you find anything there you think needs to be . . . your place, you t-t-t-take it right down there. You understand?"

I nod and then look up at the nurse.

"You better take good care of him."

She's not looking at me; she's going over his chart. When I repeat it, she just nods a little and then looks up.

"I need to examine Mr. Everett. Would you step out, please?"

I lean down and say, "I'll take care of the shed, Gamaliel. And I'll come back to see you. Need you back up at the house, so you make it up there real soon."

When I look back at the nurse she's waiting with an impatient look on her face. She says, "There are more patients, young man, that I need to see. Please step out and let me do my job."

For just a second I think about what Daddy would do if he was standing where I am now, and for that second it feels like exactly the right thing to do.

Then I turn and walk to the door and run into Carrie about halfway down the hall.

"Is everything all right?" she asks, a little fear in her voice.

"Everything except that nurse is a real bitch," I say, and then say, "Sorry, Carrie."

She waves it off. "I've heard worse from Pop in the last few days, believe me. She in there now?"

I nod. "Ran me out so she could examine him."

"Okay," she says. "I guess I'll give it a few minutes. Thanks for coming, Boone, I know he liked it."

"Take care of him, Carrie," I say, and realize that I've got a catch in my throat.

"I will," she says, and hurries down the hall.

On the ride home I think about what Gamaliel said to me and wonder what's in the shed. I'll need to go up there tomorrow morning, I decide, and spend some time in there. It's only about ten feet by twelve, so there's not much place to hide things.

The next morning I go up to Gamaliel's, taking Frankie with me. It's cold now, but the weather's nice and Frankie's having a great time dashing around his house, stopping by every few minutes to check on me. Then she's off again, chasing nothing in particular. I open the door to the shed and prop it with a rock, turn on the light, and stand in the middle and make a slow circle, just to get a picture of

287

the place. I've never really looked at everything that's in here before.

It's pretty clear that Gamaliel has lived here a long time. The place is packed with, well, stuff. I'm staring at the door, so I look right and walk over to that corner. Hanging on the wall next to the door is a hoe and a shovel, both with worn handles and nicks in the blades. Gamaliel didn't keep a garden anymore, but he must have had one, I think. Those tools have seen some use.

I turn away from them and face a twelve foot long wall that has shelves running the length of it, three of them, with the top one just above eye level. The floor under the lowest shelf, which sticks out and makes a kind of workbench, is stacked with paint cans, most of them rust covered, and buckets, some of them those five gallon plastic ones that stores use to sell everything from feed to paint to grout. Next to the buckets is an old water hose coiled up more or less neatly, and a pile of cardboard boxes. I decide to work my way down the wall, looking at all the shelves, and get to the boxes at the end. The only thing past the boxes is the big glass jug and funnel that I already know about. The old man and I used it to filter shine. Thinking about that makes me smile; after a second I shake the memory and turn back to the shelves in front of me. The bottom shelf has a bunch of small jars on the end closest to the door, like the ones the shine is in, but these are more or less full of nails and screws and washers and that kind of stuff. There's a few cardboard boxes with the same collection of stuff, not sorted in any kind of way that I could see, just thrown together. From there to the end of the shelf is a whole collection of hand tools — nice, but nothing special. Nothing I need to take down to the house.

The second shelf is easy; it's got a bunch of old fluorescent bulbs, some two feet long, some four. I don't remember any fluorescent lights in his house, and wonder briefly why he's got them in here and why he's keeping them. The top shelf is up high enough that I need to take a couple of the old five gallon buckets, turn them upside down, and stand on them to get a look.

Some old rags thrown in no kind of order on the shelf are hiding something in the back, all the way against the wall. I pull the rags out of the way and reach back, get my hand on it, and try to lift it. It's long, and I have to use both hands.

I get down off the buckets and go out into the yard to get into the light.

Chapter Thirty-Four

It's a rifle, but not like any rifle I've ever seen before. Like something out of a history book. I brush off the dust and sight down the barrel, then examine the trigger and workings, not knowing exactly what I'm looking for until I find it.

There's a metal plate right above the trigger, and when I get the light on it and brush the last of the dust away I see a date. 1856.

Damn, I say to myself. This rifle might be from the Civil War.

That's really all I know about this kind of thing, so I don't even try to figure it out. I know I've got something really old here, and maybe worth a lot of money. This has to be what Gamaliel was talking about.

I put it in the truck and go back into the shed.

I spend another few minutes in there, not expecting to find anything else. The glass jug and funnel and box of charcoal I put in the truck, too. The box is almost empty and I have no idea where to get any more. I need to get Gamaliel to tell me these things.

For the last time I go back into the shed and look around. The wall opposite the shelves is piled with broken stuff — old shovels, hoses that I'm guessing have splits in them, a tiller that looks like it hasn't been started for twenty years. Nothing really valuable, as far as I can see. The back wall has one of those pegboards that hold tools, and it's about half full of hammers, saws, and stuff like that. There's a four-foot level leaning against the pegboard. On the floor next to where the glass jug was is an old cardboard box, about two feet square and a foot and a half high. It's covered in dust and cobwebs and has a stack of old magazines on it. I pick up one of the magazines and dust it off. It's an old National Geographic, the date says 1977. There's about ten or eleven of them in the stack. I pick them up and set them on the floor next to the box. Where the magazines used to be there is a rectangle with no dust on it, and I can see the top of the box. No label of any kind, nothing that would tell me what was in it.

I am about to pick up the box when there is a knock on the shed door. I spin around, and Nancy is standing there with Frankie.

"Hello, Boone," she says, a little uncertainly. "Hope you don't mind, I thought you might be up here. Frankie is a great dog. Aren't you, girl?" She has her hand on top of Frankie's head and the dog looks like she's died and gone to heaven. I can't help but smile.

For a second I'm thinking I do mind, this is private, none of her business. I look up at her and think, what the hell, and I wave it off.

"No, I don't mind, Nancy," I say and nod toward Frankie. "Doesn't look like she minds, either."

She scratches the top of Frankie's head and the dog nuzzles Nancy's hand and then hears something and takes off. She steps into the shed and looks around.

"Did those two guys steal anything from in here?" she asks.

"I've been looking around, trying to figure that out," I say. "Not as far as I can tell."

"So if everything's okay, come on outside. I want you to show me where you chased off those guys," she says.

I look at her and she's backing away from the shed door and holding out her hand. I look down at the box and think, I'll get that later, and step out into the light. There's a good breeze blowing and Nancy has on a coat wrapped tight around her. I'm definitely feeling the wind through the jacket I've got on. Frankie, on the other hand, is loving this. She's bouncing around Nancy and then running off and coming back full speed and Nancy laughs and then shakes her head and looks at me.

"Boone, you're freezing. Just show me where you were standing and then let's go back down to your house and you can tell me about it there."

I take her around to the part of the yard I was standing in when I saw the thieves and she looks real quick and then says, "Okay, let's go. This wind's about to cut me in two."

It's about to cut me in two as well, so I head toward the truck; she gets in her car and backs out and turns down the hill. I get Frankie in the front seat with me and we follow her down, being careful of the ruts and bumps. I don't want to break that glass jug.

When I pull into the yard she's already standing by the kitchen door. I wave her over and hand her the rifle. Her eyes get real wide and she says, "Why are you handing me this, Boone?"

"I've got other stuff to carry," I say, picking up the glass jug. I decide the charcoal will be all right until later; no rain in the sky, and it's still early in the day. She looks at the jug. "What's that thing for?"

"Let's get inside, Nancy," I say, and she turns and heads toward the house. When we get inside I put the glass jug on the table and take the rifle from her.

"Come on in here," I say, and head for the living room.

293

She sits down beside me on the couch and I say, "Don't you want to get out of that coat?"

"Oh, yeah, I guess so," she says, and stands back up, takes off her coat, and sits back down. I hand her the rifle and point at the metal plate. "Does that mean what I think it means?"

Nancy laughs. "Silly, I don't know anything about guns." Then she looks at the metal plate, lays the gun down on her lap and wipes it with her fingers, looks at it again, and then looks up at me.

"Boone, this is when this was made?"

I shrug. "I guess so. I don't know anything about this kind of stuff either."

"But that would mean this is almost a hundred and fifty years old!"

I nod.

She hands it back quick. "Where did you get that? It must be worth a lot, don't you think?"

I sit back on the couch. How much do I tell her? I realize that I really want somebody to talk to about this, and I have nobody. Gamaliel was the one I talked to, and I didn't do that much. Now he's laid up and she's sitting right here in front of me. What the hell.

"Okay, Nancy, you can't tell anybody about any of the stuff I'm about to tell you. You have to promise."

Her eyes narrow. "Boone, have you done something wrong? Are you in some kind of trouble?"

There is no way she could possibly know about Daddy, but the question still scares me. I almost decide not to go on with this, but I feel like I'm already too far into it to stop now.

"You have to promise, Nancy. It's important."

She takes a deep breath, and then nods.

"Out loud. Say you promise."

"You're starting to scare me, Boone, but okay, I promise."

She sits there and so do I, for a long time.

"Well?" she says.

"Okay. The gun is Gamaliel's. You know he's in the hospital, right?" She nods, not taking her eyes off me. "Okay, well, yesterday I was in his room and when Carrie, that's his daughter, when Carrie left the room he said that I should look around in the shed and if I saw anything that I felt like needed to be down here instead of up there I should take it with me."

"I don't understand."

I'm not going to tell her what an asshole Jerry is, even though I think that part of what Gamaliel is worried about is him getting his hands on some of Gamaliel's stuff. "I think that he's worried ever since those guys were around trying to break into his place."

"But you told him they got caught, right?"

"Yeah, but I think he's still worried. Anyway, just before you got there, I was looking around and this was on the top shelf, way back. I think he was afraid somebody would steal it."

"Why did I have to promise not to tell anybody about that?"

I look past her into the kitchen and she turns around, looking back over her shoulder.

"What's that big jug for?"

"That's actually the part you can't tell anybody about. Remember, you promised."

She looks down for a second and then looks up at me. I realize that I'm still holding the rifle and I lean it against the couch behind me.

"Okay, so tell me the rest."

Chapter Thirty-Five

Last chance to back out, Boone, I say to myself, but I already know I'm going to tell her.

"It's what he and I use to filter shine with."

Nancy looks at me blankly for a second, and then turns around to look at the jug. Then she gets up and goes into the kitchen. I'm right behind her. She reaches out and touches the jug.

"You use this for what?"

"Well, it's not just this. There's a big funnel, and some kind of fancy paper, and something called activated charcoal. It takes a long time, it just drips through."

"You make moonshine?"

"See why you had to promise?"

"You make moonshine." She is struggling, I can tell, and I've got my fingers crossed that she doesn't run out the door. If she does, what am I going to do? I don't want to have to think about that.

She pushes past me and goes into the living room. Good, I think to myself. Good.

She sits down on the couch, and I go past her and sit down next to the rifle.

She's looking at her hands, laying there in her lap, and then she looks up at me. "You and Gamaliel make moonshine." She shakes her head and I think I see a little smile in the corners of her mouth. "How long have you been doing this?"

"Well, I haven't really made any yet, I just helped him finish a batch. I don't know how long he's been making shine. You see why you had to promise? It's not just my secret, it's his too."

She nods. "I get it, Boone, I do. But nobody makes moonshine anymore. They all cook meth or grow pot."

Nancy is really smiling now, and I feel everything loosen up. I was so tense, waiting, not knowing what she was going to say or do. When I look up at her she's looking at me like she's waiting for me to say something.

I don't know what to say, so I keep quiet.

Then she says, "So can I try it?"

"Really?"

She laughs out loud, and I start laughing, too, and it's a nervous laugh, a I-don't-know-what's-about-to-happen laugh, and a laugh that drains all the tension out of both of us, and then I stand up and head for the kitchen. She's up and right behind me, and when she sees the jars she starts laughing again.

I take down the one I've been drinking out of, it's about two-thirds full, and set it on the counter. Pointing to the cabinet over the stove, I say, "There's glasses in there. Get us a couple, will you?"

She picks out two small ones and puts them down next to the sink.

"I'll get you something to mix with it," I say. "You want water, or an S&S?"

"Whatever you're having," she says, a little uncertainly.

"I was just planning to drink it straight," I say, "but that's probably not a good idea for you."

She picks up one of the glasses and holds it out to me.

"Pour," she says.

She has no idea, I think to myself. I'm tempted to pour it full, or at least half, but I don't want to waste the shine. I figure she'll take one sip and toss the rest of it into the sink or out the door. I pour a tiny bit into the glass, fill mine about a third full, and she follows me back to the living room.

"That's a lot," she says, pointing at my glass.

"Not really," I say, "I just gave you a little so you could taste it. You might not like it."

"I probably won't," she says, "but only one way to find out."

I raise my glass to her like I've seen on TV and realize I'm nervous. Was this a good idea? What if she gets sick? What if she goes home and tells her parents? What if she can't drive home? I remember the first time I tried shine it knocked me back, but I had more in my first swallow than I gave Nancy in her glass, so I should be okay. So if I'm okay, why am I so scared?

While I'm sitting there worrying, Nancy is taking her first taste.

She takes a sip and her eyes widen.

"Is it supposed to burn like that?"

"I asked you if you wanted a soda or water or something. Gamaliel says it's no good unless it scratches like a tomcat all the way down." I take a drink, maybe a little bigger than usual, just to show her how it's done. My eyes water a little, but I pretend everything's fine. She's wiping her eyes and looking at what's left in her glass.

"Maybe I'll have a little soda in this."

I grin at her. "Told you." I get up off the couch and take her glass. "I'll be right back."

She grins back. "So this is why you don't come to school anymore? You do this every day?"

I haven't taken the first step toward the kitchen; I stop in front of her and think for a minute.

"Nah, not really. I don't come to school anymore because it's boring and nobody gives me any shit for not going."

Nancy frowns a little. "I don't think it's boring at all. I like it."

Halfway to the kitchen, I pause and say over my shoulder, "So you going to college or something when you get done?"

When I take the last few steps and set the glasses down, I turn and she's right behind me. It startles me a little bit, but it feels pretty good having her this close. Then I'm all nervous again and I say, "So, uh, so, you said to add some soda?"

"And a little more shine, about as much as before."

"You sure about that?"

She nods. "My little brother has a ball game down in Athens and Mom and Dad always go to the games. I don't have to be back home for a while, not til seven or so."

I put a little shine in her glass, fill it with soda, and hand it to her.

"So you going to show me this pool you told me about?"

I look outside and the afternoon sun is shining, but there's enough wind to move the branches.

"It'll be cold."

She takes a sip, then a bigger one. Then she looks over at me.

"I'm not going swimming, silly, I just want to see it."

I drain my glass and say, "Get your coat."

Chapter Thirty-Six

Frankie is all around us as we walk through the woods. She knows where we're going and sure seems to like having Nancy around. The path is easy to follow, no overhanging branches to speak of, and in a couple of minutes we find the stream and follow it up to the pool.

Nancy stands at the edge, swaying a little bit. "It's really nice, Boone. I see why you like it here."

She spreads her arms out and twirls around, and she's moving closer to the edge of the rock.

"Uh, Nancy, maybe you — "

I can see that she's falling backward, toward the pool and the rocks all around it, and she's terrified, trying to get her balance, arms windmilling around and I jump toward her and slip on a rock and sort of fall in her direction.

Her foot slides backwards a half step and I'm thinking what the hell am I going to do if she cracks her head on a rock? Then I see her drop into a crouch and grab at a crack in the rock and then Frankie is there and Nancy's holding onto her collar and I get my balance back too and all of a sudden we're all sitting on the same rock just down from the place I usually sit. Just like we had meant to sit down and rest for a minute.

Nancy's breathing is starting to slow down and the panic is leaving her face. I must still look pretty awful because she points at me and starts laughing, gasping, and then she says, "You should see the look on your face, Boone! You need to take a breath or something."

"Are you okay?" I finally get the words out.

She nods. "I just lost my balance for a second, no big deal. I think you thought it was a lot worse than it was."

"What about that?" I point to her right hand. The skin on her knuckles is torn and bleeding. She looks at it like she didn't realize until just then that she was hurt.

"Guess we should go on back down to the house and let me wash up," she says. "You got any bandaids?"

I shrug and Nancy shakes her head. "Honest, Boone, you really don't know?"

"Momma always knew stuff like that."

There's an awkward silence that goes on and on and then Frankie comes up and starts nuzzling at my hand, asking for a head scratch.

"We should go let you get that cleaned up," I say, and start to turn.

"Will you help me down off this rock?"

I look up and she's holding out her hand, the one with the scraped knuckles, and I take it and hold it while she steps off. I lean over and kiss the knuckles and then, embarrassed, say, "We should get going." I look up and she's smiling at me.

Frankie goes ahead of us and we are silent down the trail and across the yard. When we get into the house, I say, "Bathroom's that way. I'll look around for some bandaids."

"I can just rinse it off here in the kitchen," she says, "but I'm no good with my left hand."

It takes me a minute, but I finally get it and step up to the sink, on her right side. I turn on the water and say, "It takes a second for it to get warm."

"You could get me another drink," she says. "Just some Thunderstorm this time. I'm feeling a little funny, I guess it's because I never had anything to drink before."

"No problem," I say, "just Thunderstorm. That feeling will go away, you know."

She nods and says, "You should check the water."

It's warm, so I take her hand and hold it under the faucet, trying to be as gentle as I can. I realize how rough my hands are, but Nancy doesn't seem to mind. When I look at her she's staring at me.

"That's good," she says. "Did you think where the bandaids are?"

"Let's see if you really need one," I say and pick up the dish cloth to dry her hand. She reaches for a paper towel and hands it to me. "Try this."

"Oh. Yeah." I take it from her and fold it twice. then start dabbing at her knuckles. There's almost no blood, just a little lost skin, and I turn the paper towel over to the dry side and use it to dry the rest of her hand.

"Thanks, Boone," she says. "How about that drink?"

"Coming right up," I say.

I pour her a half glass and some for myself. When she sees me put a little shine in mine she says, "Maybe just a drop in mine too."

"Okay," I say.

"So do you want to go into the living room and sit down?"

I give her back her glass and pick mine up; she nods and heads toward the couch.

When we sit down I'm immediately thinking of the last time we were here and how great it was until Nancy pushed me away and pretty much ran off. I look over at her and I can tell she's thinking about it too. I'm grinning a little when I raise my glass and take a sip; she does the same and then we're sitting there, I've got my elbows on my knees and my hands between them holding my glass, staring down at it.

"What are you thinking, Boone?"

I don't look up. "Thinking about the last time we were on this couch together."

"Me too."

"I don't know exactly what to do here. I don't want to scare you, Nancy, and I sure don't want to run you off. I like having you here, a lot. Not a lot of people to talk to these days, you know."

I realize I'm about to cry and think, you can't do that, Boone, act like a baby, not in front of her anyway.

There's a long silence, and then she says, "Talk to me, then, Boone. Tell me about you and Gamaliel and this shine thing you've got going. How did you find out that he knew anything about it?"

This feels funny; I know she's trying to make things easier and in one way it is, but in another way it's harder.

So I start talking, all about how Carrie, his daughter, asked me to look in on him and how she said he liked a beer every now and then and I had found Daddy's hiding place and took him a little and we got started talking. About how he showed me some of what you do right at the end but not how to get things started.

I'm just blabbing on and on and Nancy doesn't say anything. Pretty soon I feel her hand on my arm, just resting there, and I don't know whether to stop talking or not so I just keep going. She squeezes my arm and I look up and she's right next to me. I didn't even hear her scoot over.

"Listen, Boone, I gotta go home, Mom and Dad will be home real soon and I can't not be there. I wish I could stay, but they'd ground me for sure if they knew where I spent the day. Even though we didn't do anything. You understand?"

"Sure, Nancy, I get it. I wouldn't want to stick around if I was you. Not much going on here, right?"

I almost miss the hurt look in her eyes because she turns her head. "I said I wish I could stay, all right?"

She gets up and I'm up and standing next to her. I grab her arm and turn her towards me.

"I didn't mean that, I mean, I — "

She pulls away from me and starts toward the kitchen. She turns around.

"Walk me to the car?"

She's halfway to the door before I catch up to her. We go out into the yard; it's darkening, and I know she's right. She needs to get home or get in trouble.

When we get to the car she starts to reach for her keys and I step in front of her and put my arms around her, squeeze as hard as I can, and feel her arms come up and pull me into her. I lean back and so does she, and our faces are inches apart. I'm not sure, but I think I start moving first. Then we're locked together in the same kind of kiss we shared on the couch the last time, except now our bodies are pressed together and it all feels as close to perfect as I can remember anything feeling ever in my life.

I don't want this to stop, but she pulls away from me after not long enough, not nearly long enough, and says, "Wow. I really need to get out of here. See you real soon, Boone."

She steps back, fumbles her keys out of her pocket, and opens her car door. Just before she gets in she puts her hand on my cheek and says, "Don't drink all that shine, okay? Save some for the next time I'm over here."

"Okay," I manage, and can't think of anything else to say. What I want to do is take the keys out of her hand and throw them into the darkness, take her back into the house, and feel her against me again, like she was a second ago.

Instead, I watch her pull away and this time I'm not beating on her hood and making a complete fool of myself.

Chapter Thirty-Seven

It's been a couple of weeks since Nancy was over; we talk on the phone a lot but she says she's got a lot of school stuff to do. Some of the stuff she says on the phone makes me think she's about half scared to come back because of what we might do. I guess I'm a little scared too, but I won't tell her that. Besides, I'm not all that scared, mostly I'm just wanting her back up here.

I take a walk out around the barn and start to go up to the pool but turn back; it's full winter now and feels like it's always about to rain that cold drizzly shit that I hate. So I make it a short walk and head back to the house.

Frankie is sitting by the kitchen door when I get back; she took off when we first left the house and disappeared into the woods. She's finished running, I guess, and wants to come in from the cold and have a bite to eat. We go inside and I feed her, heat up the other half of the frozen pizza from last night, and sit down with a glass of shine to do something I have been putting off for a while now.

I get out all the money that I have, from all the different places, and put it all on the kitchen table. Momma doesn't send money anymore; her last letter was short and she said that Jake was not happy with her sending his money off to Tennessee, so I'm thinking that there won't be any more coming. I've managed to keep paying the electric bill, and I'm on a well, so there's no water bill. The pile of money looks awfully small.

I think about the box of money I found up at Gamaliel's place. So far I have stayed out of it, but I think I might have to change that real soon.

The old guy's always been good to me, and I can't say that about many people. I don't want to take his money, but I'm looking at a really small pile of cash and not much food in the house. Maybe, I think, I can take just a little of one of the smaller rolls and put the money back when I earn some.

Then I realize how stupid that is, since I don't have a job and sure as hell don't want to be out in the fields like Daddy was there towards the end. I saw what that did to him and I don't want any part of that. This whole thing is pretty damn depressing, and I was feeling so good just a little while ago, thinking about Nancy being here. I pour a really strong drink and I'm about halfway through it when there's a knock on the door.

Hell, who could that be? Nobody knocks on my door, except the law or that guy who came to tell Gamaliel about his dead kid. Whoever it is, I figure it must be bad. So it takes me a minute to decide to go to the door.

When I open it it's Carrie and immediately I think that she's come to tell me that Gamaliel's dead.

Instead she says, "Would you come up to Pop's house, Boone? Tell your folks it'll only be for a bit."

"My folks aren't here, Carrie."

"Okay, then, that makes it easier. Were you busy doing something or can you just follow me up?"

I go back into the kitchen and get my coat. "I'll be up there in a minute, just let me get Frankie settled down."

When I get up there Carrie calls me into the front room, the one where I first saw Gamaliel. She sits on one chair and motions me to sit. I do, and she doesn't say anything for a minute.

"You know it's going to take quite a while for Pop to get over this," she says. I nod, and she continues.

"He's going to be with us this coming year for sure and maybe longer. Jerry and I were thinking about renting the place out, but when we told Pop, he said no."

I wait, and she takes a minute before she goes on.

"Pop says that he's coming back up here, and he says for you to keep an eye on it for him. I know you're almost grown, and Pop likes you a lot. Would your family think it was awful if we asked you to move in up here, keep the place up? We'd pay you, not much, but a little every month on top of the electric bill and things like that."

She looks at me with a question in her eyes.

I take a minute to answer. It really wouldn't make any difference to me which house I was living in is my first thought, but then I think it would be nice not to be reminded of all the pain and anger and sadness every time I walk down the hallway.

"Carrie, I think I could do that, I mean, if Gamaliel wants me to keep a close eye on things, I guess I could do that."

She smiles a tiny smile. "You know he might be wrong about coming back up here," she says. There's a little tremble in her voice, but she doesn't look away from me.

I start to say something and have to clear my throat. "Yeah, Carrie, I know that."

"When I told him I was going to talk to you about this he said, 'Tell Boone the instructions are in the back of the shed, next to the charcoal.' He didn't say what kind of instructions." She looks at me with a quizzical look. "You know what that's about?"

I try to think up a lie real quick that'll explain what he said, because I think I know what he's talking about.

"Oh, I borrowed a pump for my bicycle, I guess that was the first time I really talked to him, and a couple of weeks later I was teasing him about how old his tools and stuff were, and he told me I just didn't know how to use them."

I'm kind of laughing while I'm talking, not looking over at her, and hoping she doesn't ask me anything else.

"He hasn't bought a tool of any kind in who knows how long," she says, and when I look over at her she's smiling like she's remembering something good. "He wouldn't let anybody mess with any of his things. He must have liked you from the start."

"I guess."

"Anyway, you won't mind being his house sitter? You're sure?"

What I really want to do is go up to the shed and see if what is next to the pump is a set of instructions on how to mix up the mash and use the still. Then I remember I never opened that cardboard box that was next to the glass jug and the charcoal. I was about to, and then Nancy came by, and I got distracted.

"What are you grinning about, Boone? You look like the cat that swallowed the canary," Carrie is saying uncertainly.

"Sorry, I was just thinking about, about, about a joke I heard the other day," I say, and know immediately how lame that sounds. "Tell Gamaliel I'll be glad to keep his place up for him. Tell him not to worry."

She's shaking her head at me. "I'm not sure I want to hear whatever joke you were smiling about. If I remember, teenage boys were pretty crude."

Then she laughs out loud. "Why, Boone, you're blushing!"

She gets up and walks toward the door. "I'll tell Pop what you said, and, well, thank you, Boone," she said, very serious now.

I try to get serious and mostly succeed.

"Glad to do it, Carrie."

She pauses and turns to me. "I was pretty sure you would say yes, so I put a list of phone numbers and monthly bills on the kitchen counter, along with some money. If I left out anything, you let me know, okay? I'll call and let you know how Pop is getting along, and you call if anything happens that we need to know about or if you run low on money."

"Sure, Carrie, tell Gamaliel not to worry." I know I'm repeating myself, but I can't think of anything else to say.

She nods and then she's out the door. I hear her car start and pull out onto the road, and she's gone.

I look around. This'll probably be a better place to spend the rest of the winter, I think to myself. Gamaliel took a lot better care of his house than Daddy did, and besides, if Daddy's not working in the fields, there'll be somebody new in that old place next spring anyway.

There's not much in that place I want to hang onto; I guess I'll pack up my clothes and some of Frankie's stuff, and definitely get the shotgun and shine and Gamaliel's rifle out of there, and the boxes from the pool, but I really don't want anything else. I hope Momma got everything she wanted out of there. I'm ready to walk away from all of it.

I'll spend tonight there, I decide, packing a little and all that, and tomorrow I"ll put everything in the truck and call Mr. Wilcox.

Then I think, why would I do that? It's not like they ever did anything for me. Maybe I'll just let them find out on their own.

I realize I won't have to worry about the school hassling me any more. Hannah's already gone, been gone for a while, and if they send somebody out to look for me they'll find an empty house and probably think I moved out of the county. This is good; it's been a while since things went my way. I figure I'm due a break.

The only person I want to know about this move is Nancy. I'll give her a call tonight and tell her what I'm doing. Maybe she'll come up to Gamaliel's house for a Christmas slice of pizza or something. Maybe I'll give her a little jar of shine if I can find a ribbon to tie around it.

Chapter Thirty-Eight

I come in the back way. Frankie's beside me,
sniffing, alert, but she settles back down and we keep
going. I haven't seen anybody at the old place in a
couple of months, but it's getting close to planting
time, and I guess that Mr. Wilcox has surely figured
out by now Daddy's not living there anymore, maybe
has a new worker and his family living there already.
Just in case, I try to move as quiet as I can. Past the
still, which I know I'm going to have to move soon,
looks like it needs some work but I don't know when
I'll get to use it again, then over by the pool, that
looks just like it always has. There's one jar of shine
under a rock right beside where I used to sit, cooled
by the moving water, and I remind myself to get it on
the way back out. The boxes I got out of their hiding
place a while back.

The last part of the trip is the trickiest; the bag is
a little heavy, and I don't want anybody to see me. I
don't want to have to explain this, not after all this

time. We edge around the barn, which isn't in very good shape, not that it ever was, and head over to the little field.

It's grown up so much that it takes me a while to find the spot, even though the spring growth hasn't really started yet. All the weeds and kudzu and new saplings are matted together. I stop at about where I think Daddy is and turn slow, looking at the line of trees, the barn, and the house, and decide that it's the right place. Not that anybody besides me and Frankie will ever know.

The stone I picked up when I was over here last week. It's a rough flat oval, about twelve inches across, and the writing is on the side that is going to face down. I'm not doing this to advertise anything. I clear away an area just a touch bigger than the stone and use the trowel I brought to scoop out a little depression so the rock can blend in a little better. I take one more look at the writing before I lay the stone in the hollow and scatter the leftover dirt.

It reads:

Here Lies Nathaniel Hammond
Husband and Father
Died Sad and Angry 2013

I take one more look around to make sure nobody's watching, and stand for a second over the stone. "Goodbye, Daddy," I whisper. "Even a mean son of a bitch like you deserves a marker."

Then, "C'mon, Frankie, let's get out of here. Carrie is supposed to call today and let us know how Gamaliel's doing." She moves toward me, and I notice she must've run through a cocklebur bush. I'll pick them out of her fur after we're off the property and back down at Gamaliel's house. I grab the empty bag and the trowel. "Let's not forget to stop by the pool, girl," I say, and we head off, around behind the barn, and into the woods.

End of Book One

Boone's story continues in "Matching Scars," Book Two in the series. Available in both print and ebook format.